She glanced at Reed and wondered if he could be the type of man to take Kyle away from here, from the people who loved him

Too complicated. Too scary.

In a perfect world, she'd ask Reed what he thought about the possibility Kyle was Jesse's and what they should do about it. In her dream, he'd tell her it would be great to have a nephew and maybe the boy would come visit when he was older, say eighteen and a half. In the meantime, he'd busy himself setting up a college fund.

That could happen. Maybe Reed Maxwell was a good man, a fine man. He certainly looked fine. The dark knit of his shirt stretched across muscle that nearly begged to be touched. His face cleanly shaven did the same for kisses.

Heaven help her, she needed to make her mind go someplace else.

Dear Reader,

When you read my books, I feel like a real storyteller. Thank you for that!

The past has been harsh with Abby Fairchild and Reed Maxwell. What they don't know—at first—is they can help each other mend what's broken about their lives and brighten their future.

I hope you enjoy Abby and Reed's story and that you have fun meeting more of the residents of the fictional town of St. Adelbert. Some of these characters will help Abby and Reed and some will hinder, but together these people offer color, heart and a sense of belonging.

Also get a peek at how Maude DeVane and Guy Daley—*He Calls Her Doc*—are doing. Hint: Maude has gained several "good" pounds.

I'd love to hear from you. Visit my website at www.marybrady.net or write to me at mary@marybrady.net.

Enjoy,

Mary Brady

Promise to a Boy
Mary Brady

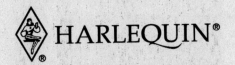

TORONTO • NEW YORK • LONDON
AMSTERDAM • PARIS • SYDNEY • HAMBURG
STOCKHOLM • ATHENS • TOKYO • MILAN • MADRID
PRAGUE • WARSAW • BUDAPEST • AUCKLAND

Recycling programs
for this product may
not exist in your area.

ISBN-13: 978-0-373-78436-3

PROMISE TO A BOY

ABOUT THE AUTHOR

Mary Brady lives in the Midwest and considers road trips into the rest of the continent to be a necessary part of life. When she's not out exploring, she helps run a manufacturing company and has a great time living with her handsome husband, her super son and one cheeky little bird.

Books by Mary Brady

HARLEQUIN SUPERROMANCE

1561—HE CALLS HER DOC

To my husband and son who appreciate me on
many levels and on most days.

Acknowledgements

To my critique group: Denise Cychosz,
Pamela Ford, Victoria Hinshaw, Laura Iding,
Laura Scott and Donna Smith who freely
offer their wisdom and encouragement.

To the people of Montana
who have allowed me to build a fictional town
in their beautiful state.

And last, but never least, to Kathryn Lye,
my editor who helps me focus on
giving my readers the best story.

CHAPTER ONE

"You're not Angelina Fairbanks."

"I knew that." Abby Fairbanks smiled at the man who had rung her front doorbell—insistently—interrupting an excellent game of Candy Land with her nephew. She brushed a clump of dark curls out of her eyes so she could get a better look at the tall and sullen stranger.

He studied a photo in his hand and then looked at her again. His dark brown eyes gave nothing away, but his frown deepened. "This is supposed to be the address of A. Fairbanks who moved here from Denver. Is Angelina here?"

Abby reached out and tipped the edge of the photo so she could see the image. It was Lena all right, from a few years ago when they lived in Denver, and it looked as if it had been taken at one of the parties during which her sister had partaken of more than one mood-altering substance.

She looked up at him and gave him a long steady not-quite glare.

"I guess that would depend on who you are." *And what you want with my sister, mister.* He didn't look like the law, thankfully, because Lena had cleaned up her act.

The man eyed her suspiciously.

Abby fingered a button at the V of her flowered Henley-style shirt and then tugged down the edge of the hem that must have flipped up when she sat on the floor playing with five-year-old Kyle. When she realized these twitchy actions probably made her look less confident than she wanted to look, she put one hand on the doorknob and stood up straighter.

"What do you mean, it depends on who I am?" he asked.

The man's rumpled blue-and-white-striped dress shirt had a small drop of something red—ketchup hopefully—on the front of it, and the quilted leather bomber jacket he wore looked high fashion, or rather...well, she'd think girlie if he didn't look so hot in it. Whoever he was, he had traveled far away from home.

"Montana's a big state and St. Adelbert is a small out-of-the-way town. We don't get many strangers here, especially on our doorsteps. It makes us cautious." Abby hoped the nudge acted like a warning shot fired over his head.

"It's important that I speak with Angelina. Is she here or not?" He widened his stance to look more intimidating. He didn't need to. His muscular body and deep frown were enough for that.

Abby suddenly felt something she hadn't felt since she moved back to the small town of St. Adelbert.

Fear.

What if there was something in Lena's past she didn't know about, something bad enough to have some city man chase her down?

"I'll be back in a few minutes, sweetie," she called over her shoulder to her nephew, who no doubt was already getting anxious to continue their game. Then she stepped out onto the dull gray porch badly in need of paint and pulled the door closed behind her. She was safe outside. In a town this size, where everyone loved to know everyone else's business, all she needed to do was call loudly and at least three neighbors with weapons of some sort would converge. Even if it was just one of the gray-haired women across the street with a cast-iron skillet.

The man stepped back toward the wooden railing. His short dark hair looked as if it got the tender loving care of a city barber, no, make that a stylist. His nails were neat and his skin, probably a pale shade before he left home, had been cast with a pink tinge from exposure to the harsh mountain sun.

Things could go any which way. She could push and he could push back harder. She took a deep breath and decided the best thing to do was to keep things light, until he did something to actually threaten her or hers.

"If you're a bill collector, she's out of the country. If you're the police, she didn't do it. If you're a suitor…" Which Abby definitely knew he was not. Her sister would have told her about any hotties she had on hold. "She said I should stand in for her."

She gave him an impeccably polite smile, hoping that last little bit would scare him off. It would most men who preferred her pretty, vivacious sister, with the flowing auburn hair and bright blue eyes.

His dark brows pulled together. He must be trying to figure out which of the options he was. She almost chuckled, but stayed silent. Let him fill the void.

A few long seconds passed. This man wasn't a very good void filler because he just stared back at her.

She held her smile.

He didn't smile at all.

"Where is she?" he finally asked.

Before Abby could respond, the door behind her flew open. She spun and bent over her five-year-old nephew, putting her body between the man and the child. The boy looked up at her with his big blue eyes, her sister's eyes. "Aunt Abby, can we finish our game now?"

She put her hand on his blond head, curly hair like hers, not straight like his mother's. "Go back inside, Kyle sweetie."

"Who's out there?" Kyle tried to see around her, but the big city had taught her caution on the border of paranoia, and where Kyle was concerned, everyone was to be suspected first. Trust needed to be well earned.

Abby physically turned Kyle around and pushed him gently into the house. "I'll be in very soon. Why don't you pour us each a glass of milk, and I'll get cookies down when I come in."

"Yippee, cookies," the five-year-old shouted as he ran toward the kitchen at the back of the house. A cookie bribe. The bad-aunt police should be after her any minute.

"And pick up your toys," she called after him and then slowly pulled the berry-colored front door closed again. When she turned back to the stranger, he suddenly seemed taller, stronger, and she needed him away from the house, away from Kyle. She stepped off the porch and down onto the sidewalk bordered with unruly wildflowers.

"I'm Angelina's sister. Who are you and what do you want with her?" she asked as he descended the steps.

"My name is Reed Maxwell." He didn't offer his hand. She probably didn't look as if she would accept the offer.

"Maxwell as in Jesse Maxwell's relative?" One of the *rich snobs?* One of a *bunch of people who didn't care about anyone except themselves?* Those were the kinds of things the man who rented the living quarters above her garage had said about his family.

"Jesse's brother."

"Of course you are. He has a picture of your family, though it's several years old." Like about a decade or so. The brothers in the photo were gangly teens. This one had definitely developed a man's body. "Jesse hasn't changed much."

Reed Maxwell nodded. "I wanted to ask Angelina if she knows where he is. According to what I found out in Denver, she knew Jesse when they lived there." The words sounded like an accusation. Maybe Jesse was right. Snobs.

Light. Keep it light, she reminded herself. "He...um...said none of his family gives... well, he said something about...a rat's ass, about...none of his family giving one... sorry...about him."

The man smiled and brought one hand up to rest on his hip under the lower edge of his jacket.

Of all the things Abby expected from him, a big grin was not it. Some of the tiredness lifted from his face, brightening his whole appearance and making him—well—yummy.

"What," she asked, jerking her wandering mind away from thoughts of yummy, "are you smiling about?"

"I know I'm on the right track. The 'rat's ass' hyperbole would be the kind of thing Jesse would say about us." He put the photo in the inside pocket of his leather jacket. "And he's probably right for the most part, but I do need to speak with Angelina or Jesse if you know where he is."

"Angelina's not here. Neither is Jesse."

"Jesse was here? In St. Adelbert?"

For almost a year. How could a family not know where one of their own was for that long? "He lived, lives above my garage in the apartment there."

"With your sister."

"Angelina doesn't live here."

"So, do you know where Jesse is or when he'll be back?"

Her shoulders drooped when she thought of her tenant. "I wish I knew. He just sort of disappears sometimes. He's been gone for over two months this time."

"And that's different?" Reed Maxwell shifted one foot up onto the lower step. Dress shoes, those slim, well-fitting ones that spoke of money—with laces and everything—and a scuff on the toe of one. A very long way from home. Chicago, more precisely, a rich suburb north of Chicago according to Jesse.

"I haven't heard anything from him," she explained. "Not that he usually calls and he never writes, but I thought since he's gone so long he would have let me know he's all right. Has he called you in the past couple months?"

The man shook his head thoughtfully as he rubbed his fingertips along his jawline where a long day's worth of dark whiskers grew. "Are you sure Jesse and Angelina aren't together somewhere?"

"Angelina is out of the country. Jesse said he was going hiking in Utah, but that was only supposed to be for a couple weeks."

"And you didn't think to contact his family." His grin had long since left and the tiredness returned.

I hope you're not this rude when you're well rested. "I sent a letter two weeks ago to an address I found in his things. I haven't heard a peep in response."

"Even though you believed we didn't give a—care?"

"Make up your mind, please. I should write. I shouldn't have written. Jesse's a friend of my sister. She's worried and so am I. I did talk it over with the sheriff."

"And?"

"Well, the last time Jesse went missing for almost a month and I was about to go file a missing person's report, he showed up. I told him about it and he got really sad, asked me never to do that. So this time the sheriff said to give Jesse time. I was going to wait till I heard from his family before I did anything, um, rash. For all I knew he was home in Illinois."

The man looked out over the mountains rising beyond the town. Then he looked back at her and almost drilled through her with his dark eyes. "I'd like to check out his apartment."

She involuntarily took a step back, her heel coming down in a clump of white yarrow releasing the stringent, musty smell of the injured plant.

"I don't think I can let you in without Jesse's permission," she said as she stepped forward to take back the ground she had given.

He must have realized he was coming on strong, because he put up a hand in a conciliatory gesture, an uncalloused hand that had never held a rope or the reins of a workhorse. "I don't mean to cause trouble. I'd just like to find my brother. How much back rent does he owe you?"

"Why do you think he owes money?"

"Some things don't usually change much over time."

"Three months." And the edge of financial oblivion lived a constant threat right under her toes as compounding interest worked heavily against her. The last three weeks...

"I'll pay the three months and I'll pay for next month. Will that buy me entrance?" He reached in his pocket for his wallet. Not a wallet, a money clip, of course.

She couldn't meet his probing gaze without a chance to think. She turned away to study an old red pickup passing slowly in the street. She had no idea how she planned to find the mortgage payment due three weeks ago, and her SUV was also late for an oil change. The house needed work and Kyle needed clothes that would fit, and soon. School started next month.

"It feels mercenary," she said quietly. *Or worse,* she thought. Their mother had said again and again that taking money from a man without good reason was wrong. On top of a winning personality, Delanna Fairbanks did have some morals. "With Jesse missing."

"And you need the money."

She swung back to face him. "What makes you think I need…"

He pointed at the sagging corner of the porch roof.

Abby pushed the blowing curls from her face again.

"My sister promised to live here and to pay rent." Now Abby had only the income from her nurse's job at the town's one medical clinic. "And Jesse was never very good at paying rent on time."

She could turn him down, or because she had always cared for Kyle and seen to his needs, she could swallow her pride and do what needed to be done.

"You can get Jesse to pay me back," he offered.

She looked into his eyes and thought she

saw a hint of amusement. They both knew Jesse wasn't going to pay his brother back.

"Okay," she said, feeling as if she was betraying Jesse while Jesse's brother peeled hundred-dollar bills off the wad without even asking what she charged.

When she took the cash she realized it was more than she thought. "This is too much."

"I'm sure Jesse has cost you more than what I've given you."

She found herself smiling. "He does have a way of making his problems seem like mine. And he has such an innocent way of doing it."

The man's expression lightened again. Maybe he was remembering the delightful, funny way his brother had of being irresponsible.

"Um, the door's not locked," she said. "You can let yourself in."

"So I could have walked in and you'd have had to get the sheriff to stop me if you didn't like it."

"You could probably walk into many places here in St. Adelbert—" he gave her a skeptical look and she continued "—but you would not want to cross our Sheriff Potts."

He nodded and turned toward the garage located on the other side of her side yard.

Abby watched his confident stride. He walked as if he were used to getting what he wanted. He probably never disappeared for weeks at a time and never in his life let his hair and beard grow long like Jesse's—though he might look good with longer hair. In fact, he'd make a great wild mountain man. She imagined him wearing buckskin pants and maybe one of those shirts made of rough cloth with an open V-neck, open down to his navel. Instead, even a bit disheveled, he looked sleek, smooth and, she'd wager, was totally out of his element in Montana. Wild mountain man...

Ridiculous. He probably followed rules and regulations all day long. Heck, he probably made those rules, but was he really a snob who didn't give a rat's behind about his brother? He must care a little. He was in St. Adelbert searching for him.

Abby let herself back into the house. He could check the apartment and then there would be nothing to keep him here. He'd go to Utah. Maybe he'd find Jesse and let her know. She liked Jesse. It was more like she had a younger brother as well as a younger sister when Jesse and Lena were around.

She wondered, as she picked up a pair of Hot Wheels cars, if there was anything in Jesse's apartment to find. Jesse may be a wayward fellow, but he always seemed so open, a no-secrets kind of guy. And she'd never found anything odd or even telling lying around when she tidied his apartment and put away his clean laundry. Jesse Maxwell had no secrets that she knew of anyway.

REED HURRIED UP THE STEPS to Jesse's apartment two at a time. He had been trying to find his brother for six weeks, first on the internet and by phone, and last week he started in person, and now he had a real lead.

The apartment door opened into a kitchen, with a dining and a living room area as one continuous room, one continuous *small* room. He could see a bedroom and bathroom through the open door off to the left.

Everything was in order and clean. Not a thing out of place. He wasn't sure what he expected, but neatness was not it.

So not like the drop-it-anywhere Jesse he

had known. The place was as orderly as his own condo, and he couldn't imagine living any other way. Jesse could and did. Helter-skelter best described the life the Jesse he knew led. Maybe miracles did happen.

Reed pulled out his mobile phone and ran his finger across the screen to boot it up. Two bars. Good enough.

He needed to speak to his business partner. Corporate investing seemed to go better when his and Denny's complementary brains studied the deals together. Denny looked at things more from the people angle and Reed from the logistics side. Together they understood better than most the motivations and financial implications of buying businesses and real estate for their business clients.

But right now, Denny was also working on a personal issue for Reed.

Reed placed the call.

"You found civilization. Impressive," Denny said instead of hello.

Reed laughed. "I wear my battery out checking for service."

"Find anything out there, and where is *there* anyway?"

"I'm in St. Adelbert, Montana. Cheery

little burg buried in the mountains where my brother has an apartment."

"But no pay dirt?" Denny was perceptive.

Reed looked around and then decided the bedroom might be the best place to start searching. As he neared the bookcase along one wall, he stopped for a moment. On the top shelf sat the photo of him and Jesse with their parents Abby had mentioned. That Jesse had it was a wonder. That he displayed it made him think Jesse might not hate his family as much as he pretended.

"Reed?"

Reed moved on. "But—he's not here. Hasn't been for a while, a couple months."

"Then you won't want to hear that your mother has been in again asking if you found anything."

"I wear out the rest of my battery listening to her voice mails." He opened the top drawer of the beat-up old dresser and picked up a paltry pile of cancelled checks from the local bank.

"I told your mother I'd call her if I heard anything from you."

"Thanks, I know it won't stop her from

coming into the office and I promise I'll make that up to you some day." The checks were mostly to Abigail Fairbanks in nice, neat penmanship, only the signature was Jesse's. The memo lines said rent, cleaning and laundry. That explained why the apartment was so neat.

"Don't think I haven't got things figured out, buddy." Denny's tone held a mock challenge.

"What's that?" Reed played innocent.

"Your mother is the reason you went out there instead of hiring someone else to do the legwork."

Reed gave a gruff sound that probably passed for laughter. "Might have been. I need you to see what you can find on Abigail Fairbanks. She's renting an apartment to Jesse." He gave Denny the address listed on Abby's checks and then moved around the things inside the drawer to look under them. A few pairs of new underwear and some unmated socks, one with a hole in the toe. Nothing else.

"Related to Angelina? Oh, and I know it's a little late, but I found Angelina. She's in the army. Apparently, she was given a strong recommendation by a judge to find some meaning in her life."

"Sounds like Jesse's type. Abigail is Angelina's sister." Angelina was apparently a wild woman. He wondered what Abby was like. Her mass of dark curly hair, warm brown eyes, snug-fitting flowered shirt with its seductive V of buttons and jeans said she had a figure that probably drew a crowd of men. People in Denver had been happy to regale him with stories about Angelina, whom they called Lena. None of the neighbors knew much about Abby, not even her name.

"From what I can tell, Angelina hasn't been in any trouble since she left for Fort Jackson, South Carolina. She's in the Middle East right now."

"Do they have any other siblings?"

"Not that I've found."

"Angelina might have a child. A little boy came to the door when I was talking to the sister. He called her Aunt Abby and she called him Kyle."

Denny laughed. "Are you sure the child is a boy? Many gender related names are crossing over to the other side these days."

Reed made an exasperated sound. "Who

am I to know? I've paid so little attention to kids in my life, it could have been either, and I probably wouldn't have been able to tell even if I had seen the kid's face."

Denny shuffled papers. "Wait. I think I have info about a child, but the sources, apparently a bit on the drugged-out iffy side, said—yeah." The paper shuffling stopped. "They thought the kid was a little boy and might even have belonged to the sister. They rarely saw him. The sister took care of him anyway."

Reed pulled on the handles of the second drawer. The drawer stuck, but when he pulled harder it opened only to contain a very old pair of jeans and a couple T-shirts, each with a rude saying.

"Maybe the kid lives with the aunt because Angelina isn't mother material." Much like Reed's own family. One brother stayed and made something out of himself, turned the family misfortune around. The other brother couldn't be bothered with responsibility, family or otherwise, and just disappeared into the West. And then there was their mother...

"There's more." Denny rustled more papers.

"Seems to be some confusion because they are both A. Fairbanks."

"Go on." The next two drawers were empty. Again a reflection of his brother's life.

"Apparently their Denver departure was rather abrupt and it might have had to do with the sister and not Angelina."

Reed put his free hand flat on the dresser top. "Any details?"

"I'll see what I can find out. I assume you don't want me to tell your mother any thing."

"That'd be correct. Thanks, Denny."

Reed hung up and crossed the room to where a wood-framed picture sat on the bedside table. The photo was of Jesse, Angelina, a toddler and Abby and it looked to be a few years old. Abby looked serious and the others were grinning. The kid was probably the child on "Aunt" Abby's porch. He picked up the snapshot. The boy looked familiar, but maybe that was because all kids looked the same to him, they just had different colored hair.

He placed the picture back on the table and continued searching. There was nothing in the bathroom except a dry, cracked bar of soap and a neatly folded towel. On top of the refrigerator in a basket was an old letter from their mother ranting and raving in the tone of a chronic alcoholic. This would be the address Abby had used. It was their summerhouse in the Chain of Lakes area and no one was there this year. The letter would probably arrive in Evanston soon and the housekeeper would forward it to Reed's office in Chicago with any other mail that might upset his mother and contribute to a relapse into the bottle.

Where the hell are you, Jesse?

ABBY TOSSED TOYS INTO the wooden "pirates treasure" box while Kyle ran to get a new game, undoubtedly leaving another mess on the floor outside the game cabinet as he tried to decide which one. There was nothing left of the cookies but crumbs and Kyle had beaten her at most of their half dozen games of Candy Land.

All the time they played, she wondered if she had done the right thing, letting Jesse's brother into the apartment. Legally, she supposed the apartment wasn't Jesse's anymore. He hadn't paid the rent due before he left, he kept meaning to and now his brother had.

Maybe Reed would find something she didn't know about and get a clue as to where Jesse had gone after Utah. A stab of dread hit her as she thought of something happening to Jesse.

She picked up a picture of the four of them. It had been taken at the zoo in Denver and she'd had a copy made for Jesse. They were so young in the picture. Lena had just turned eighteen when Kyle was born and he was barely two in the picture.

Abby always wondered about Jesse and Angelina, how their relationship went.

"Is Mommy scared?" Kyle stood, holding the Shoots and Ladders game.

Abby put the picture back and smiled at Kyle's sweet face.

"Maybe she is sometimes." She handed the photo of his mother in uniform to Kyle and he left a kiss print on her face where he'd placed so many others. "But she's in a place where there are a lot of people to make friends with. I bet she misses you a lot, though."

"She left her bunny slippers. Do you think she misses them?"

On Kyle's feet were large pink bunnies with floppy ears and black button noses.

"I think they look great on you," she said, and smiled.

He grinned and then his expression grew serious enough to wrinkle his forehead. "I'd be scared."

What did she say to that? She couldn't tell him not to be scared, but she could listen.

"You'd be scared?"

"If I had to go and live with strangers."

She reached for him and pulled him into a hug. "I don't think you'll have to worry too much about that, you rascally rabbit slipper wearer. You've got me and your grandma here."

She tweaked his nose and he grinned again.

"Do you promise, Aunt Abby?"

"I promise," she said with as much animation as she could stuff into her tone.

The doorbell rang. In the reflection in the hallway mirror, Abby could see Reed Maxwell silhouetted in the sheer lace curtained window of her front door.

"Is that the man again?" Kyle wiggled out of her arms. "Can I see him this time?"

"I want you to stay in the house. I don't really know this man. He's a stranger." And he's poking and prying. She wasn't sure she even wanted to know how he found out that Lena and Jesse were friends. And if he found that out, how much else did he know? And what did he plan to do with that knowledge?

"We don't like strangers. Do we?" he said in a serious little-boy tone.

Abby tugged one of his blond curls. "We want to be safe around strangers. That means you stay inside right now. I'll put a DVD in if you want."

"Land Before Time. Land Before Time."

She popped in the kid dinosaur DVD as the bell rang again.

"I'll be back in a few minutes. Please stay here."

He gave her a half nod, already holding the remote control in anticipation of the movie starting.

Ah, if life were that simple.

Now all she had to do was send Jesse's nosy brother away and she could watch the movie with Kyle. She should clean the bathroom and address a few cobwebs, but she wanted to spend as much of her day off with her young nephew as she could. Being a nurse at the only clinic in St. Adelbert didn't leave her much free time.

Abby opened the door and this time stepped out onto the porch to greet Jesse's brother. "Did you find anything that would help?"

"There's not much there."

"Rolling stone and all that. It's too bad he's not here. If you had come in the spring…"

He seemed as if he was trying to decide something. Maybe he just wanted to make sure he asked all his questions before he got back in his rental car and left town.

"I'll give you my phone number and if you think of anything else, you can call me. Anytime." Abby felt an urgent need to reassure him and send him on his way.

His brow furrowed.

"I don't mean… I mean I'm not trying to get rid of you," she hurried to say and then to prove her point she sat down on the top step and invited him to sit. His brother was missing, after all. There had to be some middle ground between the bum's rush and trying to keep Kyle's and her little world undisturbed.

He declined to sit, but descended and put

one foot on the lower step as he had earlier. He was tall, and sitting, she did feel at a disadvantage. Maybe that was good. Let him think he had the upper hand.

"Do you know where in Utah he went hiking?"

"There are several parks—Zion, Grand Canyon, Bryce Canyon and more—but he didn't name one specifically."

"Do you know if he went hiking alone?"

"He usually did. He said it gave him the space to think."

"Was there anyone else in town Jesse was friends with?"

"Maybe, but he didn't confide in me. Like I said, he and Lena were friends. She lived in the house with me for a little while."

He nodded toward the house. "Is that little boy Angelina's child?"

Abby turned to see Kyle peering out the window beside the door.

CHAPTER TWO

ABBY FOUGHT BACK THE sudden sensation of panic, an immobilizing dread that had first started when she had been trapped on a dark night by reporters. She had thought she'd banished the feeling forever. She swallowed and quickly stuffed it into the bad memory file where it belonged.

Kyle waved at her. The boy had to move the plant and stand on his tiptoes to see out the lowest window in the column beside the door, his nose pressed on the glass probably leaving a mark. She motioned him away and he disappeared from view.

When she turned back, the thoughtful look on the man's face appalled her. There were no reasons for him to be interested in her sister's child—none she could possibly acknowledge anyway.

Abby suddenly didn't want to talk to Reed Maxwell anymore. She didn't want to talk to anyone about her sister's child, except her sister. Her mission in life right now was to protect that little boy. She'd been doing it since before he was born and she'd do it as long as necessary, forever if she had to. The best way to do that was to send Jesse's brother back to Chicago.

The sooner he left the better, because there were questions she had asked her sister about Kyle and hadn't gotten any satisfactory answers, answers about Kyle and Jesse. It hadn't seemed very important before, but with Lena so far away and this man here asking questions, she recognized how little control she might actually have over what happened to Kyle.

Reed Maxwell had to go. Now. Because he was beginning to make the safe town of St. Adelbert not seem so snug anymore.

"If you leave me a contact number, I'll email my sister again about Jesse, and I'll call you and let you know what she says, and if I hear anything from Jesse, I'll call." She sounded flustered. She knew she did. Maybe he wouldn't notice.

He half turned away and then turned back. "I thought, until I can be sure I've found out everything I can from the people here about where Jesse might be, I'd stay in Jesse's apartment for a few days."

"Stay in Jesse's apartment? You want to stay here in St. Adelbert?" A wrenching, gut-level protest flashed through Abby. This man could *not* stay in town. There could be no good reason for him to stay. There was nothing for him here.

He stared steadily, silently. Unsure she could say any more without sounding like a crazed shrew, she did the same.

The adrenaline rush and the late-afternoon's cool breeze made her skin prickle. She couldn't have him digging into Kyle's past, her past, and if he stayed, he might do just that—until he discovered things he did not need to know.

"If there's a chance I can find something out about Jesse by staying here for a couple of days, I'm going to stay."

She watched his face for some kind of hope that he was kidding, pulling her leg. City Man Invades Small Montana Town a Hoax. Ha ha! We always gotta have hope, her mother would say. But there had been no give in his words, and now no relenting in the expression on his face.

The bottom of her world gave way a bit.

Okay, then. She made herself relax and smile. "If I can do anything to help, let me know." She had to keep him from discovering for himself the things about her sister and Kyle that Lena would never clarify, but that could no longer be ignored or treated lightly.

Was Jesse Kyle's father? If he was, did Jesse know or even suspect?

Pudgy-cheeked and blond, Kyle was nothing like the dark and lanky Jesse and if Lena had not wanted to tell anyone, Abby had known it wasn't any of her business. It wasn't until her sister went into the army leaving Kyle in her care that she had admitted she should have insisted on concrete, believable answers, but pinning down her younger sister was like holding fog in the palm of her hand.

Jesse's brother climbed the steps and sat down beside her. She stayed where she was, refusing to give an inch.

With the tip of her fingernail she flicked off a chip of the peeling gray paint. The flake landed with a tiny click on the sidewalk below.

Maybe Reed thought she was being friendly. The niggling of dread threading through her thoughts told her it was more likely he could see through her facade. He knew she wanted to send him over the mountains never to come back again, and in protest, he was staking a claim.

She held her ground.

"I have this mother, you see," he said quietly and then fell silent. He didn't seem to be expecting her to comment. Instead, he gazed intently out over the neighborhood.

Abby sat silently. Let him ponder. It was a dirty trick to bring his mother into this. She didn't want to hear about his mother. She didn't want to think of Jesse's family, have them become human beings and not just the miserable caricatures Jesse had sketched and then dismissed.

What did a man from the flatlands see when he looked out over the neighborhood? Did he see the houses, the white clapboard, the stone and the log-cabin wannabees, all stout enough to withstand heavy snows and each sheltering a family with their own story?

Did he see the trees, some as old or older than the town and each planted by the wind, the squirrels, or human hands? Surely he had to see the mountains in the distance, hazy and ancient, and some would say full of mystery and lore. Always mountains. Beautiful mountains that kept the rest of the world at bay—most of the time.

How had this day gone from playing Candy Land to feeling as if she had been hurled off the top of the Gumdrop Mountains?

Instead of pressing her for information she did not really have, Jesse's brother's broad shoulders drooped.

She wanted to reach out and comfort him.

She scrunched her hands into fists. Always the nurse. She could not comfort the whole world and especially not this man—the one who could be the enemy. Kyle came first. She needed to protect him. *I'd be scared... If I had to go and live with strangers.* Kyle's words chilled her.

What if it came to that? What if Reed Maxwell came for his brother and settled for a boy who might be his nephew? What if he knew for sure about Kyle's heritage and had come for his nephew in the first place?

No matter what, he couldn't just take Kyle away without cause.

What if he had cause? What if he knew why she had fled back to St. Adelbert?

Abby cringed, but then she put the thought away. She had to. She was getting ahead of herself. It could be Jesse was not Kyle's father at all, and her sister just kept the man close because she liked having a fan club. That was not at all beyond her sister, but if Abby believed that, maybe she believed the moon was made of green cheese, too.

Reed had a missing brother and he had a mother, who probably missed her son. Nursing had taught Abby almost everyone had feelings for one of their own.

Whatever Jesse and Lena did was not this man's fault nor his mother's, and what lived in Abby's past was Abby's alone. She couldn't tell Reed he had a nephew because she didn't know if he did, and it would be unfair to give him and his mother that kind of hope.

Nor could she feel good about sending him away. Again, there had to be a balance point somewhere between the compassionate human being she should be to this man and the vigilant protector she felt she had to be when it came to Kyle.

She bowed her head. "Jesse hires me to do his cleaning and laundry. I just cleaned his apartment and washed the sheets again a couple days ago. I can repeat the cleaning and do the laundry before Jesse gets home."

"I can pay you, better than Jesse did." The man didn't pull his gaze from the horizon. "Hell, Jesse could pay you better than he did."

"You've already paid me enough." She tucked her fingers under her thighs. "Tell me about your mother."

"A piece of work."

"She must miss Jesse if she sent you looking for him."

He gave a short bark of laughter at that. "My business partner accuses me of coming out here to look for Jesse so I could get away from my mother. He might be right."

"You ran away from your mother?"

"I know how this sounds, but she used to be a nice, tidy drunk who never bothered anyone."

Abby turned and leaned her back against

the decorative post so she could see him better. The look of regret on his face said he wasn't kidding about his mother, either.

"Jesse didn't talk about your mother much, not specifically, or any of you. He seemed content to think of all of you as some distant, vaguely related people, and he didn't seem to need to have any of you in his life."

"I don't think any of us can blame him for that, but last year our mother sobered up, and eventually she realized she'd been drunk almost her whole marriage, for sure most of the time her sons were growing up."

"That must have been hard on you and your brother." As dear and funny as her mother was, Abby knew what it was like to be ignored by a parent.

"When we were younger it was hard. Once we were old enough, it seemed like an advantage. We mainly got our way, any car we wanted, parties at the house, apartments of our own at too young an age."

"What about your father?" Since she had hardly known her own before he ran away, Abby found herself wondering about other people's fathers and how they related to them.

"He's probably exactly as Jesse described him. He was either gone or negotiating with someone and couldn't be bothered with his family."

"Ouch."

"Kids can survive a lot."

"Jesse said he was cut off from the family because he didn't conform." She wanted to say *to their idea of what a human being should be.* She might be prying, but if Kyle's happiness depended on her knowing what kind of people Jesse's family were, then she had to dig.

"I suppose, in a way he was. Jesse was cut off from a paycheck he wasn't willing to work for. He has a trust fund he never touches and prefers to do his own thing, be his own man. My rebellious brother, the cliché."

"That is so Jesse. He tries hard to be different from his family, or his idea of what his family is like or what any family might be like. Sometimes he could be a real pain and sometimes he's just cute." Abby smiled at the thought. "As long as he was free to move about, without any real entanglement, he seemed happy."

"Our mother wants to see him. I suspect

she wants absolution or something. She wants the family she never really noticed before. Maybe she finally deserves her family, her children and who knows, maybe grandchildren some day."

Abby didn't know what to say to that. His brother was funny and often irresponsible and now he was missing. A dread grew inside her. If Jesse was Kyle's father, what would his family do? They had money. Money often spoke louder than signed papers. Would they try to take the boy, take him to Chicago and make him live, afraid, among strangers?

Abby wanted to shriek at her runaway imagination.

But she needed to consider all the possibilities, not let herself be blindsided, not again. She wouldn't let Kyle down and she wouldn't let Lena down now that her sister was trying so hard to reform in the army, to grow up. And Abby knew she couldn't do anything to keep Reed from looking for his brother, but she couldn't sit here any longer catastrophizing, either.

"I hope Jesse comes back soon, for your mother's sake."

"She'd appreciate it."

"Well, I have things to do," Abby told him, pushing up from the step. Things that didn't involve getting to know this man or his history or encouraging him to hang around St. Adelbert.

Or taking a chance on spilling things she didn't know if she believed herself, like Jesse and Lena possibly having a child together.

REED STUDIED THE WOMAN standing over him. Her riot of dark brown curls swept along her jawline and somehow seemed perfect for the angles of her face. She was attractive in a natural, unmade-up fashion. Her figure was tantalizing. But her eyes struck him the most. They flashed light brown, almost yellow like the color he imagined a mountain lioness's eyes to be.

He stood and faced her. He had no business noticing her eyes. "Thanks for your time."

"I hope your mother gets to say whatever she needs to say to Jesse."

"I shouldn't have bothered you with my mother. I have no idea why I did. Tired, I guess. I was in Denver yesterday."

"You drove through the night from Denver? You are tired."

"I suppose I look pretty bad." He brushed his hair back. There was a little extra to push around, as he was a couple weeks past his usual cut. "I slept somewhere in Wyoming, but not long."

"Well, I wouldn't say you look bad, but you do look tired. I wish I had answers for you, but I truly have no idea where Jesse might hike in Utah or where he might have gone after he left."

He could see the unsaid "if" in her eyes. He believed her. She was skittish and protective of the boy, but there was an open honesty in the way she presented herself, something missing from most women in his life, for that matter, most of the people in his world. Something that must have made him feel compelled to spill out his history to her. Yeah, he was tired.

"I have a few things to do, too, people to talk to. I found a couple uncashed checks and paycheck stubs in Jesse's apartment. I guess I'll start with those people."

"You might want to get some sleep first."

The door to the house popped open, and they both turned to see the boy come charging out like a small bull.

"Aunt Abby. Aunt Abby!" he called in the high-pitched tenor of a small child.

"You rascal. Is the movie done already?" she asked as the boy stopped just before crashing into her. She leaned over and scooped him into her arms and stood. He grinned ear to ear and when he did, a big dimple showed in one cheek.

Reed hadn't missed the look of alarm on the woman's face when the boy opened the door. He hadn't missed the look of love, either, as she clasped him in her arms.

"Gramma's on the phone and she said to go out and tell you to stop 'gnoring her."

She shot a look at Reed and rolled her eyes. "I have to go. I have a mother, too."

"Ask her if I can come to her house, please, please, please," the boy said with one small hand pressed to her cheek as Abby carried him up to the door. She turned and gave Reed an uncertain wave before disappearing into the house.

He couldn't help but wonder if she were for real. She seemed so, well, nice, and she could carry a forty-five-pound child as if he weighed five pounds and she seemed to enjoy it. Definitely not like most women in his life.

He headed back to the apartment to retrieve the addresses he should have brought with him. Very tired. The sooner he found Jesse, the better. If he brought his brother back home for their mother to apologize to, his part would be finished. He could get back to running his business. His partner could feel as if he had a partner again.

Abby Fairbanks thought his brother was cute. He hadn't thought of Jesse as cute— ever. He was only two years older than Jesse, and had missed being aware of Jesse's cute stage, maybe because he was too young himself at the time.

Who would know? Some long-gone nanny?

Reed thought of the smiling face of the little boy who had come running out of the house. The boy was cute also, not that Reed usually noticed such things; kids didn't play much of a role in his life. When the boy had come out onto the porch, grinning, he had that same familiar look about him. Though all little blond kids looked alike to him, this one was definitely the kid in the picture on Jesse's bedside table.

ABBY SENT KYLE TO TALK to his grandmother for a couple minutes while she wrung her hands, gnashed her teeth and wondered. How far should she have pushed her sister to find out if Jesse was Kyle's father? More important, would Kyle gain anything by knowing right now who his father was?

And then there was her mother's latest crisis—finding a husband, preferably one for her daughter and one for herself. There was always some urgent necessity in her mother's life. Usually Abby felt like the only sane adult member of her family. Today, even that was iffy.

One thing she agreed upon with her mother was the light Kyle had brought into their lives. Her mother turned uncharacteristically responsible when Kyle was around. If Delanna Fairbanks kept it up, she might actually figure out she was all right by herself just the way she was, and so was Abby.

Kyle giggled in the other room. Abby sighed. She had to talk to her mother sooner or later.

When she went into the living room the phone was missing from its usual spot on the low wooden table beside the window. She didn't see Kyle, but the chocolate-colored thermal drapes, which had been pulled back to let in the summer light, fluttered in the still indoor air.

She sneaked up and called softly into the fabric. "Boo."

Kyle squealed with delight and pulled the curtain away from his face. "Aunt Abby, you got me. Bye, Gramma. Here." He shoved the phone at her and tore off for wherever it was a boy went when the adult in charge was busy on the telephone.

"Finish picking up your toys," she called after him and then said into the phone, "Hi, Mom. I didn't give a single thought to going out with you and the undertaker guys."

"Liar, liar." Her mother laughed on the other end. "You've been doing nothing but thinking of ways to turn me down. The Fullers are such nice men and I think they prefer to be called funeral directors."

"Yeah, well. There's always hope you'll come to your senses and realize I'm old enough to choose my own dates."

"You might be old enough, honey, but you're not willing enough. Anyway, that's not why I called."

"Thank God!" Abby perched on the arm of the chair by the window.

"I'll be thanking God when you're not an old maid anymore."

"Gee, Mom, I love you, too. Why did you call if it wasn't to point out my short-comings?"

"Oh, I called about that, too."

"Mother."

"Lighten up, Abbs. I called to badger you into letting Kyle come and stay with his be-loved grandmother for a few days."

"*Beloved grandmother*—that would be you I take it?"

"You're a very funny child. I know it's weird, but I love being his Gramma."

"He's that kind of kid."

"So, can he come?"

Abby knew this would happen one day. He already stayed with his grandmother while Abby worked and if she ever had a life, her mother offered to take him all evening. Even all night, her mother had said with a sly grin. Kyle did love his grandmother. He took to her the first time he met her and she might be where he inherited his charm.

"How about Saturday, the day after tomorrow? He has a birthday party to go to in the morning and I'll bring him over afterward." Abby purposely kept the anxiety out of her tone. Letting go was hard, but she had to do it eventually. They probably wouldn't let her room with him in college.

"Hallelujah and praise the Lord," her mother almost shouted into the phone. "Saturday would be great."

"And, Mom, you'll probably hear soon enough, but Jesse's brother is in town."

"Well, that is a surprise. Talk about a dysfunctional family. If what Jesse said is true, they make us seem sort of normal. Is he looking to see if Jesse left any money behind for him?"

Abby thought of the expensive, if rumpled, clothing Jesse's brother wore.

"I don't think so, and I'm not so sure Jesse was right about his family, at least not all of them. The brother seems to be, well, normal."

"Does he know where Jesse might have gone?"

"No. Apparently they haven't heard from Jesse in over a year."

"Yup. We're the normal ones."

"I don't know if I'd go that far."

"So what's the brother like and what's his name?"

"His name is Reed Maxwell and he's tall, dark, handsome. Not my type."

"You're killing me here, kid. What's not to like about this one?"

"Hmm, let's see. He lives in Chicago and I don't know much about him for starters." Except that he's sexy and...never mind.

"Is he too rich for you or something?"

"He might be." *He might also be Kyle's uncle.* That would stop her mother cold.

"Why's he here in St. Adelbert?"

"He seems to be truly concerned about his mother. She wants to see Jesse badly." For reasons her mother didn't need to know. What Reed told her didn't seem to be appropriate grapevine fodder.

"So the mother loves her kids, and they might not be so bad after all. Are you done dodging my question about the under-takers?"

"I thought they were funeral directors,

and you haven't worn me down enough." At least she had dropped the subject of Reed Maxwell.

"A mother wants better for her children." The tenor of her mother's voice dropped and so did Abby's desire to be flippant about the subject. Her mother did want better for Lena and her.

"I am grateful for that," Abby said.

"Grateful enough to go out to dinner with me?"

"And?"

Her mother sighed in an exaggerated manner.

"And Kenny Fuller and his son, Travis. Come on, Abby. I think becoming a nurse turned you into a fuddy-duddy."

"Let's see. You mean since I learned how to take care of myself and didn't need a mother to get dates for me?"

"Stop that. All right, if you really must know. I can't get Kenny to ask me out and I'm afraid he'll say no if I ask him. This valley is so small, I can't waste a chance like that. But if I tell him that we can get the two of you to go out if we go along, he'll say yes. He has to—you're a great catch."

"Mother!" Abby found herself comparing Travis Fuller to Reed Maxwell and her enthusiasm for the double date diminished even more.

"Yeah, Mother, that's me. Kenny's a nice, respectable man. Both of them are, and if he gives me a chance, he'll find out I'm a different woman than I was when we first lived here."

"You're a good woman, Mom. You always were."

"You have to say that. You're my kid. Have you heard from Lena?"

"Not since the email I got last week. I'll let you know if I hear anything." It had actually been twelve days and Abby wondered if it was time to escalate to worry. "And I'll drop Kyle off in the morning tomorrow as usual and pick him up when I'm finished at the clinic."

"I'll see you, and maybe I'll get a date planned while you're at work then."

"Don't do it on my account."

"Goodbye, you ungrateful child."

"Bye, Mom."

Abby put the handset in the cradle, sat back and folded her arms across her chest.

She wanted to ask her mother if Lena had ever talked about Kyle's father, but knew it would do no good. If Lena had said anything, their mother would have said it didn't matter or it wasn't important. That's what she had always told them when they asked, demanded, or even begged her to tell them about their father. He packed up and left when Abby was six and Lena was a toddler. The last thing Abby remembered about her father was him yelling at her mother about having to spend too much money on a kid for Christmas, more specifically, the doll Abby had to have.

She thought about Reed and Jesse's parents. She at least had one good one, not perfect, but good.

After a few moments, she turned an ear to the house. Quiet. Way too quiet.

"Kyle?" When he didn't answer, she called louder. Still no answer. He had to be outside.

She stopped at the kitchen window and looked out into the yard. Reed Maxwell stood on the top landing of the apartment stairs, watching something below. A perplexed, contemplative look skewed his features.

Abby leaned closer to the window to see

what he was looking at. A deer? A flock of wild turkeys? A bear?

Whatever it was, it was out there with Kyle.

CHAPTER THREE

ABBY FLEW OUT THE BACK door without another thought and stopped abruptly on the back porch. No deer or turkeys or bears. No fascinating or dangerous wildlife at all. In the shade of the tree, in the sandbox, Kyle sat pouring sand into his big yellow dump truck.

Abby studied Reed on the landing outside the garage apartment. The look of speculation on his face suddenly made sense.

He knew.

Reed Maxwell knew or at least suspected Kyle might be his nephew. He acknowledged her presence with a nod and then glanced down at his phone.

Abby wanted to tear across the yard, grab Kyle and run as fast and as far away as she could, but she stayed where she was, holding her breath. If she overreacted now she might stir up something that was best left untouched. Maybe he didn't suspect anything about Kyle and Jesse, but a strong reaction from her might start Reed on a path he might otherwise not have thought to tread.

She figured he had gone on his fact-finding mission in St. Adelbert, although it wouldn't have done any good. If any of the townspeople knew anything, they would have spoken up, if not to her, then to the sheriff, and Sheriff Potts would have told her.

What if Jesse's brother pressed her for information about Kyle? Could she lie? Tell him she had no ideas about Jesse and Kyle?

Kyle played on, oblivious to both adults.

What she would not do was run. She had run in the past—more than once—from St. Adelbert to the big city. When the big city beat her down, she ran back to the small town, dragging her sister and Kyle with her. Her sister in turn convinced Jesse to come to the St. Adelbert Valley where the four of them lived for a short while in a loose family-like structure.

Abby had even bought this house in an attempt to anchor them all here, for all the good it had done. If St. Adelbert wasn't safe, where in the world was?

She chanced a glance at Reed.

Backlit clouds played at the tops of the mountains behind him as the sun had already begun making its way down into late-afternoon sky. He lowered his phone and reached up to push his hair back. He seemed to be trying to make a decision. To get closer to Kyle for a better look? Snap his picture? To grab the boy and make a run back to Chicago?

His phone rang. He gave it a look of distaste, and then he thumbed the screen, stepped back inside the apartment and closed the door.

Abby huffed out a breath of relief and Kyle filled his dump truck with more sand. He was a dear child, the perfect mix of sweet and rambunctious. Imagining life without him in it, even for a little while, had her rubbing the ache in her chest.

"Kyle, sweetie," she called and when he looked up, "come on in. We'll go get a present for Angus's birthday party."

Kyle jumped up, flinging sand from his clothes.

"Is it today?" His voice squealed with the

glee of a five-year-old anticipating his best friend's birthday party.

"No. Today's Thursday and the party is Saturday. Can you figure out how long that is?"

His face scrunched up and he silently began to mouth the days of the week as he held up successive fingers. His face lit. "Thursday, Friday, Saturday. Three days."

Abby knew in Kyle time that was correct.

His life was simple, gloriously simple, and she hoped she could keep it that way. Hoped she could keep her promise to Lena to "keep my boy safe while I'm gone."

"'S'go!" He grabbed her hand with a sandy one of his own.

IN THE APARTMENT ABOVE the garage, Reed held his phone a few inches away from his ear while Maxwell and Anderson's newest and possibly most lucrative client vented.

"I don't see how they can say they'll sell that piece of land to us and then say they won't." His client's voice blasted. It was dinnertime in Chicago. Why wasn't this man at home bothering his help?

With part of his brain Reed listened, knowing it wasn't, as the man said, about the property. It never was. It was about power and who would have the upper hand. The other half of his brain, in the meantime, tried to sort out the possibilities about his brother and the boy playing in the sandbox. When he saw Kyle hunched over the dump truck looking determined, the familiarity about the boy clicked inside his head. His look and his mannerisms reminded him of Jesse as a child.

Reed pinched the bridge of his nose as the client went on about what he kept referring to as the "untenable position." It didn't seem to make a difference what nationality, what business, or what deal, the stakes in their purest form were about who would keep or gain the power and the control.

"There is always a solution," Reed assured the man.

"We need to meet in person, if not tonight, then tomorrow morning."

"I'm not in Chicago right now."

"What do you expect me to do? I'm going…" And the rant continued.

Grow up first and second, go learn not to parry a feint. The seller wasn't really retracting the offer. He was pretending to attack his opponent's position, *pretending* being the key word. They might as well be princes fencing for the fair maiden's honor. It was no different.

"Denny Anderson already has you penciled into his calendar," Reed said when the man took a breath. "He thought he might need some one-on-one with you tomorrow. I'll have him call you in the morning."

Mollified, the man thanked Reed for his time, and, he wheezed out, "prompt attention to the details."

Denny had warned him about the tenuous situation the land deal was in, because their private investigator had dug deeper than people usually did and found the seller had title question on the land involved in the prospective sale. The bluster was a delay tactic.

Almost down to the minute Denny had predicted when the seller would seem to renege and their client, the buyer, would be calling in a panic and had assured Reed he'd see the man.

He was lucky to be in business with Denny, who thrived on converting the ridiculous to the sane.

Reed tucked his phone into his pocket and snagged Jesse's paychecks and stubs from the kitchen table where he had left them. The good people of St. Adelbert who had hired his brother were out there waiting to talk to him.

And now it might all be more complicated. Was it possible Jesse was a father?

More likely Reed was so tired, he was inventing things in his head. Surely Jesse wouldn't have gone off for two months and left his son behind. Surely Abby would have said something about Kyle being his nephew. His head ached.

He looked at the top stub in his hand. The address read "Miller's Hardware Store" on Main St. in St. Adelbert. Small town advantage. No GPS needed.

He yawned and looked over at the welcoming bed with the sheets Abby had washed. Abby, witty, attractive, maybe sexy if she weren't trying so hard to be…what…nonchalant? He yawned again. Suddenly grilling the town's merchants right this second lost its appeal.

Abby was right. Sleep was definitely a good idea, maybe not even a choice, but only for the next few minutes, a power nap. The last thing he could do was waste time. If he talked to people today, he could be on a plane for Chicago tomorrow morning and be back in the office by late afternoon.

He stretched out on the bed. He had no idea if Kyle and Jesse were related, but he couldn't help thinking a grandchild would soothe his mother's conscience. Maybe even give her the strength and courage to get outside herself and give up her downward spiral once and for all. Get her off his back. He was sure he was going to hell for thinking such a thing about his mother, and he was a bad, bad person to wish his mother on a small child.

He called Denny and left a message about the client. Then he yawned, rolled over on his side and inhaled the fresh smell of the linens. Abby must have hung the sheets on the line outside. He vaguely remembered one of the nannies having done the same thing routinely in his family's backyard, despite how the flapping scandalized his mother.

He let his eyelids close for a five-minute nap.

"CARRIE, YOU OLD CREEPFACE, aren't you ever home?" Abby left the identical message for her friend in Denver as her friend had left her—only the names were changed—and smiled as she hung up the phone. Carrie was a dear and the only person in Denver she still carried on a friendship with.

With no one to talk to, Abby washed the dinner dishes. From time to time, she peered out the kitchen window into the near darkness. The apartment above her garage, the paid-for apartment above her garage, was dark and stayed dark all the time she was washing and drying. She had been able to keep Kyle from being too curious about the man by shamelessly distracting him with a shopping trip and a long visit to the nearby park. He was safely asleep now, as apparently was the man upstairs. Thank goodness.

She put the last dish in the cupboard and pulled the whole-grain bread she had made out of the oven, placing it on the rack to cool. Then she went in to the back room to turn on the computer. Her sister wasn't online and was probably asleep somewhere. She wanted to yell at her sister for being irresponsible, for leaving Kyle in such a precarious position.

If Jesse was Kyle's father, and if Jesse never came back, the boy would never get to know his father. If Jesse wasn't his father, Kyle might never know the other side of his family. Ever. She knew what that was like. Her father's relatives had never contacted her and Lena after their father left.

Or the other side of Kyle's family, no matter who they were, might take him away.

The thought of giving up Kyle tore at her, and not just because it would leave her alone in the world with only a mother who kept trying to take husband-hunting to new levels and a sister on the other side of a very large ocean. Kyle was five and he didn't deserve to have his world ripped apart because of the adults surrounding him.

Sanity got the better of her and she sent off a cheery email to Lena about their mother and the Fuller men and told Lena she'd save Travis Fuller for her if she wanted him. She asked again about Jesse's possible whereabouts and signed off. She would do anything she could to keep her sister safe, even if that meant doing what she had to do at home and keeping quiet about the problems.

What would the older brother do for the younger brother? How far would he go?

THE NEXT DAY, AFTER HAVING slept in, Reed called his partner, Denny, who gave him a proper amount of harassment for missing their usual early-morning call. He'd told Reed all had been quiet from his mother so far, and that Abby Fairbanks was a nurse who worked at the medical clinic in downtown St. Adelbert. The Avery Clinic named after its now retired founder. The only clinic in town, so it wouldn't be hard to find. He wondered if her leaving Denver had anything to do with a nursing job.

After a shower and shave Reed jumped into the rental car and headed out to find the people whose names and addresses were on the paychecks and stubs Jesse had left behind.

He wound the rental car through the neighborhoods and pulled to a stop at Main Street. The town was roughly linear and flanked by mountains and deep green forests. A small shallow river flowing through the town dictated any bends in the streets, a river he suspected that was neither small nor shallow when the snow in the mountains melted in the spring and early summer.

To the right on Main Street sat a Chevron

station, a miniature trading post-style meant to attract tourists. He turned left onto Main Street in front of the post office, equally Old West-looking. Past the post office and disrupting the linear flow was the town square with businesses around the perimeter.

But it was Alice's Diner down the street past the square with its white paint and bright blue trim that caught his eye, more correctly, it caught his stomach, which growled loudly. Since he was soon going to need more than the mountain air to keep his coffee-addicted eyelids open, a big breakfast suddenly seemed like a great idea.

He pulled to the curb beside the diner. It was possible someone in there knew something about Jesse's whereabouts.

"Mornin', darlin'," a waitress with a lot of black hair, a white frilly apron and a name tag that said Vala greeted him as he stepped inside. "Seat yerself wherever you want."

Reed did so and turned his coffee cup right side up. A moment later the same waitress filled the heavy old mug with coffee and handed him a menu.

"I'll be back in two shakes to take your order."

It was almost ten-thirty on a Friday morning and only two other tables were occupied. Each of the eight diners, four at a table, had a cup of coffee in front of them and a platter of sweet rolls in the middle of their respective tables, a midmorning snack. Breakfast for them had probably been hours ago.

All were gray-haired, if they had hair, and each studied him in their own way. There were a few smiles, one from a woman whose checked apron covered half her denim skirt. A frowning man, a real cowboy type, looked really old, maybe late eighties, and had a deep tan on the lower two-thirds of his face, while his forehead was much lighter. Two other women—sisters? twins?—dressed alike except for their individual color theme, glanced at each other and at him and then grinned broadly.

Reed gave a simple wave. Some waved back, others nodded, and then they all turned back to their conversations. Well, at least they didn't chuck coffee mugs at his head. Not all small towns were receptive to strangers.

After Vala took his order Reed stood, and with coffee cup in hand approached the closest table. The occupants shifted their gazes up to him, and three of them picked up their own coffee cups so as to be equally armed. He smiled at that.

"You're Jesse Maxwell's brother," the aproned woman said.

So much for wondering if they knew who he was. "I'm Reed Maxwell."

"The guy at Abby's place," said one of the near-twin women.

"Sit down," a big, grizzly bearded guy said, and they all shifted their chairs until there was a space for him. Highly unusual human behavior if you compared it to the near stranger-phobia he was used to in the big cities he frequented. He liked this friendly behavior. It was—nice, he thought as he sat down.

"And don't let them get to you. They talk about all of us," the grizzly guy continued, and then he peeked over his shoulder and grinned at the women.

The women at the other table and grizzly guy all laughed together, like people who didn't always need words to communicate. Like old friends.

"I'm looking for my brother and I thought I'd ask around in here if anyone has heard anything about where he is or where he planned to go."

The phone near the cash register jangled and the waitress hurried to answer it.

"You one of them Chicago folk, too?" asked the grizzly guy. "I'm Fred Nivens, by the way. I own the auto repair shop and tow truck in town. Jesse worked for me—"

"Fred, it's for you," Vala, the waitress, called from across the diner. "And you better hurry up."

Fred leaped up so fast the pleasant-looking man next to him had to make a grab for Fred's chair to keep it from flopping backward to the floor.

"Hi, I'm Bessie Graywolf," the woman with the checked apron said as she pushed the plate of sweet rolls toward him. "Don't mind Fred. Some emergency or other is always happening at his place."

Over near the cash register, the man spoken of was gesturing emphatically as he talked into the phone.

"Nice to meet you, Bessie," Reed said as he turned his attention to her.

Fred returned to the table a moment later, but only to grab his hat.

"What's the matter, Fred? That guy from Jersey set the place on fire?"

Fred's eyes just got bigger. "I gotta go."

"Poor Fred. If it's not one thing it's the next with that darned shop of his," one of the women at the other table said as Fred rushed out the door.

Bessie leaned toward Reed in a conspiratorial manner. "Jesse only worked for Fred one month. Something about no auto aptitude, according to Fred."

"Did my brother cause trouble in town?"

Instead of shifting looks, the table broke out in grins.

"That boy is a dear," the woman across the table said.

Good. If the townspeople liked Jesse, it might be easier to get information.

"Now," Bessie said, "go on and have a sweet roll."

When Reed's stomach accepted her offer of a sweet roll with a loud growl, Bessie laughed and pushed the platter closer.

The roll was warm with some sort of dark jam inside and Bessie pointed at the couple on the other side of the table and continued. "This is Rachel and Jim Taylor, they own

Taylor's Drug Store. Over there is Curly Martin from the Squat D Ranch." The old rancher gave a quick nod of acknowledgment.

She continued, also naming the local funeral director, and the pair of similarly dressed women who ran the boardinghouse, which incidentally had no boarders right now. The pair gave him extra bright smiles and he wondered what that might be about. Reed listened to the names and bits of information and put them away where he could draw on them when he needed. He greeted them with smiles, stood and shook offered hands and then relaxed down onto the seat of his chair. Every one of them seemed, if not entirely warm and fuzzy, at least cordial.

"We all knew Jesse. He sort of wandered in and out of our lives," Bessie said as she signaled Vala for more coffee all around.

"He was such a card," one of the women who were probably sisters said, and Reed was sorry to say he had forgotten which was Cora and which was Ethel.

"Is that bad or good?" he asked.

The sisters laughed and together said, "Both."

"He'd forget he was supposed to do a job

for us and then he came and did it and then insisted we weren't supposed to pay him, cause he said it was a mitzvah, whatever that is."

"I think he meant he was doing a good deed," Reed replied.

"Yup, he was a card," Cora or Ethel said. "Remember that dog he tried to adopt and the dog just wanted to run around free and not belong to anybody?"

Both tables of people laughed and Reed got the feeling no one was laughing at Jesse, just about the story.

"I didn't know whether to feel sorrier for Jesse or the dog," the old rancher Curly Martin called out from the other table and then guffawed until he coughed and one of the sisters had to pound him on the back.

The waitress poured coffee all around and when she brought his breakfast, she brought his flatware and water from the table where he had originally sat.

"Thanks, everyone. I appreciate your Jesse tales. I just hope they aren't too exaggerated."

Several of them chuckled and the rest grinned and Reed continued. "I'm trying to find out where he might have gone and I wondered if he said anything to any of you, or if you'd heard anything."

Many heads shook.

"You're best bet for information might be John Miller over at the hardware store. Working there was the last real job Jesse had before he left," one of the sisters said.

"Do you need him for anything in particular or are you juss lookin'?" Curly asked. The drilling look of inquisition he gave Reed seemed contagious and soon they were all looking at him as if he were going to foreclose on all their homes.

Sometimes there was nothing that would suit better than the truth. "Our mother needs to see him."

Bessie Graywolf pinched her lips together and shook her head slowly. "I know that one—my daughter, been gone over a year."

Reed looked directly at Bessie.

"Sorry, Bessie," he said and was surprised to realize he actually meant it.

As his reward for acknowledging Bessie's pain, seven expressions lightened collectively. In some circles, mothers carried a lot of weight.

"Any other suggestions?" Reed asked.

"You might ask at the sheriff's office," Jim Taylor offered. "He fished with a couple of the deputies."

A couple more names were mentioned, but they were "out of town anyway." Reed shoveled food into his mouth as he listened and nodded his thanks.

The door to the diner opened and a big, blond young cowboy strode in with his hat in his hand.

"Baylor!" Several of them greeted the young cowboy as if he were an anticipated family member. Bessie motioned Baylor to Fred's empty chair. "Reed Maxwell, this is Baylor Doyle. The Doyles own the Shadow Range Ranch and Bay is one of our very own volunteer firefighters."

Baylor's eyebrows drew together as he studied Reed. "Jesse's brother. The one staying with Abby."

Reed recognized the challenge and decided it would be best to sidestep it. "Abby was nice enough to let me stay in my brother's apartment for a couple of days."

Baylor nodded at the people in general. "I can't stay. Just came for some coffee."

"I thought you were moving outta town, boy," Curly called from the other table.

"Soon, Curly, soon, you old buzzard," Baylor responded affectionately.

As if on cue, Vala set a to-go cup in front of Baylor who handed her a few dollars, snatched a sweet roll and stood with the roll balanced on top of the coffee and his hat in his other hand. "Abby is good people," he said to Reed and strode out the door.

"Baylor's right about Abby," Bessie said and chortled. "And I wouldn't cross him if I were you."

"Warning noted." He studied each of them and they all seemed serious.

"And they're watching." Bessie jerked a thumb at the other table.

The pair of women waved. "Hi, neighbor. We live across the street from Abby."

"Good to know." Reed finished off the last few bites of his breakfast.

"Yup, your best bet today is to head down to the hardware store." Bessie chased sweet roll crumbs from her apron with a sweep of her hand.

"You've all been very helpful." Reed passed out his business cards, paid his bill and tipped

Vala for every darlin', honey and sweetie pie because he could and because no one in the coffee shops in Chicago's Loop used endearments like that. Then he bid them all thanks and goodbye. When he stepped outside the sun had warmed the day to toasty and the sky was the biggest and the bluest he'd ever seen.

He took a big breath of the clean air just for the novelty of it. He'd be back to pollution soon enough.

The people of St. Adelbert had drawn him a picture of Jesse. They liked his brother, foibles and all. For some reason that meant a lot to Reed. Could just be that he was glad he wasn't hunting for some reckless brother who didn't deserve to be found. Could be he was remembering how much he and Jesse had loved and depended on each other as kids and was missing his brother.

He stepped off the curb. The redbrick building called Avery Clinic sat perched back from the roadway across the street. A sheriff's squad car parked under the awning at the front entrance was the only outward sign of life at the clinic. Must be a slow day. Might be a good opportunity to go in and ask the people there about Jesse. Abby might be there since her car was gone when he'd got up, but he was less sure about Abby since he started wondering about Kyle and Jesse. Did she have a secret the town didn't know about?

He strode up the ramp and at the top, the glass-and-aluminum doors popped open allowing him entrance. There must be a parking lot out back somewhere because inside, the clinic was hopping. In the waiting room off to the side were several adults and three very loud children. One of the men was trying and failing to control the kids. One elderly woman sat rocking back and forth as if all the noise and activity was soothing to her. If Reed had to guess, he'd say she had turned off her hearing aid. A child's shouting and screaming came from the treatment area beyond the closed double doors.

A side door opened and another family poured in to raise the clamor to chaos. A man in scrubs emerged from the treatment area and intercepted the new arrivals. He spoke with the parents and with the injured child. Then he asked them to add themselves to the crowd in the waiting room.

Two firefighters, probably volunteers like Baylor Doyle, the cowboy he'd just met in the diner, strode out of the patient treatment area and hurried out toward the door. Two of the boys from the waiting room chased after them and their father hurried after them.

A woman at the reception desk looked up and gave Reed a large PR smile. "May I help you?"

"Maybe, Arlene," he said, using the name on the tag on her blue uniform.

"I'm Reed, Jesse Maxwell's brother."

The receptionist nodded and furrowed her brow as if she already knew who he was, but was willing to let him spin his own tale or even hang by his own rope.

"Is Abby Fairbanks here?"

He looked up when the double doors to the patient treatment area popped open. Abby emerged accompanied by the sheriff, the very big sheriff. Tall and broad, who made Reed, who didn't consider himself so, feel small. The man's gaze took Reed in. An eagle would have nothing on this man.

"There she is." The receptionist nodded toward Abby and her, for all intents and purposes, bodyguard.

Reed smiled and Abby gave him a tentative smile in return.

The radio on the sheriff's belt squawked. He hefted it to his mouth. "Sheriff Potts," he said as he walked back inside the treatment area, probably for privacy.

"Hello, Abby."

"Reed, is there something wrong?"

"Can we talk for a second?"

She nodded and without speaking led him through the doors, across an open area with two treatment rooms on either side and finally down a quieter corridor with exam rooms and offices.

"Now, what can I do for you?"

The sheriff poked his head inside the hallway. He looked at Abby, and studied Reed for another long moment, and then said to Abby, "I've got to go. We'll have to talk later or tomorrow."

"Thanks, Sheriff Potts."

He gave her a one finger salute to the brim of his sheriff's hat and gave Reed another sizing-up, then hurried away. Reed tried not to feel paranoid, but this was one of those times when he knew he was a long way from

Chicago. These people could circle the wagons and he'd get nothing from them.

Abby turned to him and repeated, "Now, what can I do for you, Reed?"

She gave him a pleasant therapeutic smile and he realized he was meeting nurse Abby. That smile made him believe she could fix anything, anything at all.

"I was over at the diner and I thought I'd stop in."

A woman, a tech her tag said, in dark blue scrubs walked by, gave Reed the once-over and turned to wink broadly at Abby. Abby waved her off.

"You were at the diner," Abby prompted.

"I met a bunch of the nice townsfolk, but they didn't have much in the way of information about Jesse."

"Well, I—"

"I don't want anything on my arm." A child's plaintive shout came from one of the treatment rooms they had passed earlier. A murmuring female voice tried to convince the child otherwise.

"Nurse Abby, we need you." The woman who had winked earlier called out to her.

Abby turned to Reed. "Can you wait a minute?"

He held a hand out indicating by all means and she walked away quickly, quietly and disappeared into the nearby treatment room.

Reed followed, hanging back a bit in the hallway. He might gain some insight into the woman if he could see "Nurse Abby" at work.

CHAPTER FOUR

"I DON'T WANT A CAST."

Reed watched as Abby sat down beside the boy, but not close enough so that he might try to scoot away, and then she ignored him.

"I don't. I don't." The red-haired, freckled-face boy of about Kyle's age sat holding one forearm in his other hand. An ice pack sat on top of the arm.

"Yeah," Abby said without looking at him. "I don't like it when people treat me special, either."

The boy frowned but didn't say anything to that.

She ignored him again and fiddled with the stethoscope around her neck as if it held great interest.

"It's icky," she spoke again. "Having people do my chores for me."

"Wadda ya mean?" The boy blew at the

hair drooping in his eyes so he wouldn't have to use a hand to push the lock aside.

The boy's mother stood in the corner biting her lips so she wouldn't grin. Reed knew how she felt. He found himself doing the same thing.

"Well, you wouldn't be able to do dishes—at all—for at least a week, maybe longer, and then maybe badly enough that your mother would take over and send you out to play. Making your bed would be out for a while, too. I hate it when that happens. I want to make my bed every day. Twice if I take a nap."

The wheels inside the boy's head were turning.

"And the colors. Did you see the colors? Looks like a bag of Starburst candy in there." She pointed at the almost neon colors of the cast samples. Nice tack, Reed thought. The boy probably didn't even notice the change from the negative to the positive.

"I'll get teased."

"Only by kids who still have to give the dog a bath."

"I wouldn't have to do that, either?"

"I like giving dogs a bath." She stopped

and gave him a sad clown face. He smiled just a little at that and she continued.

"I like it when they splash dog-flavored water in my mouth." She flicked her tongue. "Yum."

Now he giggled.

"My favorite is when they put their wet paws on my lap and drip so it looks like I wet my pants when I stand up."

The boy giggled and tried to bury it in his shoulder. He knew he was losing.

"And then everybody wants to sign their names on your cast with the special pen we give you. Then you watch the kids who still have to do the dishes, make their beds and give the dog a bath. They'll be the first to sign."

"Will it hurt?"

"It might hurt a little, but not any more than it does right now. What Dr. DeVane is going to do is sort of build your arm a cocoon—well, a cocoon with fingers sticking out." She pulled her hand into the sleeve of her jacket and wiggled her fingers out the end. He nodded in rapt interest. "That way when you do stuff it will have protection for the broken part and it can heal. In six weeks the bone will be all patched up and the cast comes off."

"Will you do it?"

"Dr. DeVane is going to do it. She's our cast expert, and maybe I'll get to be her able-bodied assistant." Abby puffed up her chest and sat taller.

"Okay." The kid mumbled the words into his shoulder.

"Hey, Sammy," Abby said as she scooted closer.

"What?"

"I'm sorry you fell off your bike and broke your arm, but Dr. DeVane will help fix you up good as new."

"Will she let me feel the baby in her tummy?"

The boy's mother came away from the corner with a horrified look on her face and right then a beautiful, very pregnant woman stepped into the room and gave a questioning look to the mother, who shrugged and nodded.

"She sure will," the woman Reed assumed was Dr. DeVane said as she put a hand on Sammy's shoulder.

Reed decided his place in this scenario

didn't exist, so he turned and walked out of the clinic. He had more than found out what kind of nurse Abby Fairbanks was and any questions he had for the clinic staff would have to wait for a day when he didn't feel like he was a kid who just watched a Hallmark movie and needed to go to his room and bawl.

In five minutes, Abby had given that little boy more love and understanding than Reed and Jesse had gotten in their collective rich childhoods. Go figure.

ABBY WATCHED REED HURRY away and couldn't help but feel relief. Since she'd seen him watching Kyle last evening, she'd recognized the two adults needed to have a conversation. Right now was not the time, because she didn't yet have the courage to even think that Kyle might have another family who might want a part of him.

Maybe tomorrow, next week, or sometime after she started collecting social security would be the right time to verbalize her suspicions.

"Hey, Abby," the tech whispered. "That man, he's the guy living at your place?"

Abby nodded. "Does anyone not know?"

The tech laughed. "It's St. Adelbert, Abby. All we do is eat, sleep, work and gossip. He's hot. Do you want him?"

"What kind of question is that?" she whispered back.

"Hey, if you don't, can I have him?"

"I haven't decided yet," Abby said. That would start them wagging, guessing, maybe even betting.

"Keep me posted," the tech said and handed Dr. DeVane the chosen color of casting material. Neon-green had been the choice, as it often was for five-year-old boys.

Abby patted a smiling Sammy on the head and left to see to more patients. He definitely didn't need her anymore. See, she didn't have trouble letting go—when it didn't matter.

REED HURRIED DOWN THE sidewalk.

That Abby had become a nurse was no wonder—she was a fixer, a very good one. He pictured Abby beside the boy, letting the child set the pace. The little boy certainly appreciated someone taking the time to understand what he wanted. Reed didn't blame his brother for hanging around the Fairbanks women as long as he had. He realized if he took on Abby Fairbanks, he would be taking on the whole town. He hoped it would never come to that.

Reed passed an office building housing among other things, a real estate office and an accounting firm. In a town this small, he wondered if the same people worked in both offices on alternating days.

Next to the office building was an empty spot of land with a sign that said Future Home of St. Adelbert Community Center, but the sign was old and worn. There was for sure a story about the missing community center. He wondered what had happened between conception and completion. Could he help?

Now, where had that thought come from?

Neither Chicago nor Evanston, the suburb in which he grew up, had engendered more than basic civic duty in him. This little town had gotten under his skin in just two days.

Past the promise of a community center was Miller's Hardware Store. Beyond that was a second gasoline station connected to a grocery store. At the very edge of the downtown area, there was bearded Fred's auto repair shop aptly named Fix It Fred's. By the look of it, not any kind of franchise and badly in need of an overhaul itself, but the tow truck sitting out front was large and shiny with lots of chrome. Reed chuckled. The place looked just like the man he had met in the diner—a little disheveled but never to be overlooked.

Mr. Miller at the hardware store didn't have a clue where Jesse might have gone nor where he might be now.

"He was a different sort of fellow," Mr. Miller said. "He'd do the job. He'd forget some things from time to time, but he was always willing to make things right even if he had to stay a little longer. I was always a bit concerned about him. He didn't seem to have any...well, he never seemed to, ah..."

"Have any goals or plans for his life."

Mr. Miller nodded in agreement.

"The only thing he ever really seemed to want was to—" Mr. Miller paused and gave an apologetic flip of his hand. "Jesse ran away from things."

"Yes. He ran away from us and we let him have his way for a long time. I just need to find him so our mother can talk to him."

"I'm sorry I'm not any help. He hasn't worked for Miller's Hardware... Well, he hadn't worked for us in a couple weeks before he left, and a couple weeks was a long time for Jesse."

"Thanks," Reed said. "If you hear anything, here's my number." Reed slid the man a business card with his mobile phone number circled on it. Then he plucked a bunch of Tootsie Pops from the display near the cash register. Kyle would like them. Then he took a second bunch. He hadn't had a Tootsie Pop in years. Maybe it was time.

"He's a nice young fellow, Mr. Maxwell. He just seemed sort of lost," Mr. Miller said as he rang up the candy.

"Thanks," Reed said, acknowledging the man's concern.

"How's Abby doing? Cam and I worry about her now that Jesse and Lena have left, that she might…well…all she has time for is work and that little boy. We're not even sure she has enough money to meet her mortgage every month."

"She just got some money that was owed to her, so she'll be okay for a while."

"Give her my best."

Reed took his purchase, nodded and walked back out into the early-afternoon sunshine.

He stopped on the corner to let a pickup truck pass in the street and examined the colorful bouquets of candy in his hand. The candy made him rethink what he was doing all the way out here in Montana. He was neglecting his business for a brother who had never given one ounce of consideration to any of his family.

But these people seemed to like Jesse. They seemed to think he was searching for something and the unsaid seemed to be that his family couldn't give it to him. Were the Maxwells really that bad? Probably.

So, the best thing for it was to get things settled. The sheriff's office was just down the street from his car. He tossed the Tootsie Pops on the seat and continued.

Maybe the deputies were there who knew about his brother, but when he let himself in, the dispatcher and the big sheriff were the only ones there.

"Mr. Maxwell," the sheriff greeted him. The big man had on a crisp uniform that looked as if he never sat down in it. There was a hat crease in his forehead. He had, at least, just taken off his hat.

"Sheriff."

The sheriff seemed as though he was expecting Reed, because he pointed to an office. Reed walked into the sparse space and waited for the sheriff to finish whatever it was he had been saying to the dispatcher. A moment later when the man walked in, Reed put out his hand.

"Reed Maxwell." The sheriff's grip was firm but not hard. The man probably knew his power and most likely wielded it judiciously.

"Wally Potts."

First name, Reed thought. He must not stand on too shaky ground.

Each man took a chair.

"What can I do for you, Mr. Maxwell?"

"I'm speaking to anyone who had contact with my brother. Word has it that Jesse used to fish with a couple deputies."

"He did at that, but they don't remember him saying anything about where he was going in Utah or after Utah." The sheriff's expression remained stoic. "How much do you know about hiking in Utah?"

"Enough to know if you go there and don't want to be found, no one will find you."

Sheriff Potts nodded. "I've already spoken with the Utah Highway Patrol."

"Abby said you had done that."

The sheriff stared for a long time at Reed and Reed took it. He was sure most people found it unnerving. If this went on much longer, he might agree with them.

"It will do you no good to go to Utah—it's a big state."

"I figured that."

"Let the people who are familiar keep an eye out for him. There are some parts of Utah where Jesse is going to walk out or he's not going to come out at all."

Reed winced at this. "I never really knew what not knowing was like before. I have to say, I'm uncomfortable with it."

"I'm sorry you're worried about your brother, Mr. Maxwell. I'm sorry for your mother, too, as I understand she's looking forward to seeing Jesse also." For the first time there was a flicker of something on the sheriff's face. "And I'm sorry Mrs. Potts brings the gossip home from the grocery store and that I listen to it, but it's the best local news network around."

"I met Cora and Ethel."

The sheriff just nodded.

"Thank you, Sheriff." As dire as what the sheriff had to say about Jesse was, Reed was convinced there was another shoe hanging in the air, probably over his head.

"Is there anything you want to ask about your brother that I might be able to tell you?"

"I trust there is no reason to believe Jesse never left the St. Adelbert area."

Stoic still. "It's a fair question and the fair answer would be I can offer no guarantees on that, but I can tell you Jesse wasn't the kind of guy to collect enemies. Even the town bad ass had nothing against Jesse and he was also in Hawaii at the time Jesse left town."

"Thank you for giving my brother as much of your time as you have." Reed deliberately left out "valuable" as too condescending.

"Jesse didn't hide that he was leaving. He said goodbye to almost everyone in town."

"I've spoken with a lot of people. I think Abby might be the only one who's surprised he hasn't come back already."

"About Abby Fairbanks."

Here was the shoe. Reed listened attentively.

"I don't know how much she's told you or anyone else has told you."

"She's pretty quiet about her personal life and her past." Reed shifted in his chair to convey his sensitivity to Abby's value as a person. "I've pretty much come to the conclusion that if I mess with Abby Fairbanks, I might as well be prepared to take on the whole town."

If a man like Sheriff Potts did such a thing, the sheriff relaxed. "She's pretty important to us."

"I watched her perform a miracle with a little boy who broke his arm."

"She's flawed like the rest of us, but she's got a talent for healing the sick and injured. And if she makes a promise, she'll keep it."

"And she loves her sister's son."

"She does that. That boy has been her life since he was borne to Lena."

Reed knew a veiled warning when he heard it and he wondered just how much the sheriff knew, how much Abby had confided in him about not only Jesse, but Kyle, too. And what could Reed say? I'll not hurt Abby? He couldn't promise that. I'll leave and stop looking for my brother so Abby doesn't get

hurt? Whether or not Abby got hurt might
not be up to him or the sheriff.

"Thank you for your time." Reed handed a
business card to the sheriff. "My cell phone
number is on there. And again, thank you for
what you are doing on Jesse's behalf."

"Let me know if you hear anything else,
Mr. Maxwell."

"I will."

The intercom on the sheriff's desk buzzed.
"Sheriff, you will want to take this call."

Sheriff Potts pressed the intercom button.
"Thank you, Sheila."

Knowing the sheriff even a short time,
Reed understood that the dispatcher would
not have interrupted the sheriff without a
really good reason.

The men shook hands and Reed left.

"This is Sheriff Potts," Reed heard as he
walked out the door to the street.

REED PARKED HIS RENTAL car in the drive-
way at the apartment. The day of interviewing
people about his brother had seemed longer
than dealing with clients in the office. Maybe
the stakes were higher when family was involved. With his last two leads out of town

for the day, Reed knew he'd have to spend another night in St. Adelbert, another night sleeping on the sheets Abby Fairbanks had washed.

He had just let himself into the apartment and closed the door when his phone rang.

"Hello, Mother."

He put the bunches of Tootsie Pops on the kitchen table and drew his eyebrows together with his fingertips. As he paced the tiny kitchen, his mother picked up from where she left off on her last phone call. It was so hard for her to be alive, she said.

"I'm glad you were up and about today, Mother," he said, grabbing on to the only thing that seemed good about her day.

He half-listened as she continued to ramble about the petty aggravations in her life.

"So what did the doctor say this time?" he asked as he caught a questioning lilt at the end of his mother's sentence.

"The doctor wants me to go out and walk around the neighborhood. What would my neighbors think?" Her voice was low and gravelly from too much booze and too many cigarettes.

"Maybe they'd think 'There goes Frieda Maxwell. Good to see her out and about.'"

"What if the doctor is wrong and it's too much for me?"

Reed heard car doors slam and went to the window. Abby and Kyle appeared below him in the yard, and he found he wanted to smile at the sight of the two of them.

He returned his attention to his mother. "If the doctor told you to exercise, she must think it won't hurt you, and if you're stronger..."

"I won't ever be stronger, especially..." A wheezy sigh pierced his ear.

Especially was bait, but he swallowed it like a good son. "Especially what, Mother?"

"Oh, I don't think I should tell you."

Call her bluff blasted inside his head. Tell her okay then and goodbye. Instead, he chose words to juggle compassion with the inanity. "I know your life seems out of control at times. Hang in there. You are strong and more capable than you think. Why don't you try what the doctor says?"

With another sigh, she dismissed his words. "Did you find out anything about Jesse?"

He heard Kyle giggling in the yard below and turned back to the window. They were playing some game that involved running and apparently laughing.

"I've spoken with some people out here, but I haven't found anything yet." It said something about his mother that she had to go on—and on—about herself *before* she inquired about her missing son. He had to remind himself she was trying life without the crutch of alcohol.

"I don't blame him for being gone. I guess I'll say goodbye, then. I don't suppose either of you will ever be able to forgive me, let alone learn to love me."

Reed paced. His mother's first goodbye was only a preamble. She'd need at least three. "I do love you, Mother. Of course I forgive you and I will call you if I hear anything."

At the sound of another shriek of laughter, Reed found himself wanting to go outside where Abby and the boy were. He stepped back to the window to watch the two of them romp.

Kyle giggled again. Abby said something to him and then took off across the yard. Kyle ran after her, arms pumping.

"Maybe I should fly out there and help you."

"No. You shouldn't do that." He squeezed the phone as if it might stop her thinking such odious thoughts. He'd never get a chance to search for Jesse if she came out here. "You should do what the doctor says is good for you."

"But, dear—"

"There's no Ritz here, remember, Mother?" He pushed the curtain away from the window to get a better view of the yard. He tried to think back to what Jesse looked like as a child.

Was it possible this was Jesse's kid?

"Oh, my," she said and coughed a bit for effect. "Fine. I guess it's goodbye, then."

"Go outside and take a walk. Or have someone take you out to Old Orchard. It's far enough away from home and no one will know you there."

He tried to remember the old photos his mother had stuffed in boxes in the upstairs hall closet. He'd like to have that box right now, because other than the dimple, impressions of what his brother had looked like as a child were all he had.

"There is a Bloomingdale's there and a

Nordstrom's. I guess I could do that, for a little bit, until I get tired."

Oh, hell, she was fifty-six years old and she sounded a hundred. Alcohol had taken a huge toll on her physical well-being, but he was afraid the psychological damage from decades of drinking might not be treated even with two visits a week to her therapist. If she couldn't come to terms with her own alcoholic parents' abuse and neglect, she might not survive sobriety. Reed recognized the sinking feeling in his gut as the fear of failure to help his mother find a reason to live. He had to find Jesse.

"I'll call you soon."

She said goodbye and thankfully ended the call this time.

Out in the yard, Abby let Kyle catch her and they tumbled to the ground together. Gales of laughter floated up to the apartment. She loved the boy, but could she be hiding the truth about him?

Find Jesse, that's what he had to do, and shake him until he told the truth about the boy.

In the meantime, he'd have Denny send him a copy of a photo of Jesse as a child.

ON HER BACK ON THE GROUND, Abby spotted Reed in the window of the apartment. That must mean it was time to go inside and make dinner or something. She scrambled to her feet and reached for Kyle, but she wasn't fast enough. By the time she caught the boy, Reed was heading down the steps.

"Hi, Reed," Kyle called.

"Kyle. Go in the house and—" Holy cow, it was too early to do any dinner preparations, like have him wash his hands. "Go in and find the Frisbee. I feel like beating you at something today."

He giggled and ran inside to meet the challenge. She had finally found a lightweight nylon tossing toy that posed no danger for the child when she tossed it at him and he did so love it.

"Hello," she said as Reed approached. Maybe he was coming to tell her he was leaving tonight, or at least in the morning. He looked better today. He looked good. He looked… Never mind.

She settled on, "You look rested."

He stopped close to her, too close for the wide-open spaces of Montana, close enough to inhale the scent of man. Close enough to want to reach out and touch his dark hair, to put a hand on his cheek, to kiss him.

She took a step away and was tempted to draw a circle around her and forbid him to enter.

"Thanks. I guess I made up a sleep debt last night." He smiled. She guessed he was making an effort to put her at ease. It put her somewhere all right and nothing was at ease.

"Mountain air. Does it every time to you city folk."

"Bottle it. You'd be rich." He gave her a big, friendly grin that made her body begin to hum.

"It's been tried, not too successfully." She grinned back and was sure she was not having the same effect on him. He looked calm, untouched by anything, even her. He had to go. She was going to miss looking at his handsome face, but he had to go. "Did you get what you needed today?"

"I didn't get anything. I have a couple more people to talk to tomorrow."

"I emailed my sister last night to see if she remembered where Jesse might go instead of Utah or after he went to Utah."

He took a half step toward her. "Abby, if the two people I have left in town to talk to don't pan out tomorrow, am I out of places to search here?"

Abby rubbed one palm against the other. It would be so easy to say, "That's right. You might as well go." Life would get so much easier if he left the little valley and never came back.

She drew in a breath and mentally kicked herself because she was going to hate herself for saying what she was about to say. "Jesse worked for some elderly folks quite a ways out of town."

"Okay. Would these people know more than the people in town?"

"Clearing some brush for the Harveys was one of the last jobs Jesse did before he left, and it's a bit on the remote side. I'm not even sure if they know Jesse is still gone, but you should speak with them."

"How do I get there?"

"Like I said, it's remote. More of a showing place, not a telling place. I could say, you start with the first road past the rocks that look like a couple frogs…but it's only a short distance past the ranch where I'm seeing a patient tomorrow."

"Is that an invitation?"

She was getting herself into something now.

"I guess it is." The words came out pretty smoothly for someone who wanted to kick herself. "We can go early afternoon, if that's all right with you."

He nodded. "That gives me plenty of time to see the people in town."

He started to turn away, but turned back. "I planned on having dinner at Alice's later. I'd be happy if you and Kyle joined me."

"We can't tonight, but thank you for the offer." She would be busy distracting herself from this man and Kyle would be busy not being recognized as Reed's possible nephew. She should have sent him to his grandmother's today.

If she and Reed were going to have to have that talk about Kyle, it'd be over the phone after Reed had gone back to the Midwest and lost interest in anything west of the Mississippi.

Jesse, you little troublemaker, come back. Lena, equally the troublemaker, you stay safe.

CHAPTER FIVE

EARLY THE NEXT MORNING Abby lay with her eyes closed against the sunshine pouring in her open window. It had been a second long fitful night of tossing and thinking and drifting off. She was actually glad it was over.

She and Reed had managed a non-adversarial conversation before she refused dinner with him, and it didn't make her feel proud of herself that she didn't welcome Jesse's brother with open arms. Part of her wanted him to leave and part of her just wanted him.

How ridiculous could she be?

She had no idea what this day would bring as far as Reed Maxwell was concerned, but she had to get Kyle to a birthday party and then she had to give him over to her mother. Then she had a visit to a patient outside town who had a knee replacement in Kalispell last week—with Reed in tow.

She opened her eyes to see Kyle standing at her bedside.

"Oh!" She laughed and gave him a big grin. It was what he deserved. "Well, good morning to you."

He grinned back.

"Is it time for the party yet?" he asked, his voice clear without a sign of sleep. She wondered how long he'd been up.

Abby laughed as she looked at the clock on her bedside table. "It's six o'clock, sweetie. The party is at eleven. Let's see. How many hours is that?"

She held up her hand and they counted off the hours on her fingers.

"Five. Is that a long time?" Kyle asked, looking perplexed.

"Not so long, and we have things to do to keep us busy. We have breakfast to make and eat, and cleaning our rooms, and packing your clothes to stay a couple nights at Grandma's."

"I get to stay at Gramma's? Yippee." He jumped up and down twice and the third time launched himself onto her bed.

"Yippee," she echoed his joy and caught

him before he could land all knees and elbows on top of her.

"How about if I get up and we have breakfast."

"Can we have butter eggs?"

"Yum. Yes, we can." Butter eggs. Kyle had named them. Apt, considering butter and eggs was the entire list of ingredients fried up in a pan. "I'll be down in a couple minutes."

"Can I call Gramma?"

Abby laughed at what her mother would say to a phone call at six in the morning. "I think we had better not wake Grandma so early. It might make her grouchy."

"Gramma Grouch. Gramma Grouch." Kyle giggled.

"Yeah, we'll tell her her new name when we see her. She'll like that, too." She put a hand on his rosy cheek, knowing she never should have said the grouch thing and hoping he'd forget it. "You go down and set the table. I'll be down soon and we'll call Grandma later."

He barreled out the door.

"And wash your hands first," she called to him as he clomped down the stairs in the very loud, but very cute canvas hightops his grandmother had bought him because they had Velcro closures. "I don't want any boy cooties on my breakfast plate."

His giggle faded as he rounded the corner and headed toward the kitchen.

She closed her bedroom door, stretched and stripped off her nightgown. With a shiver that puckered everything, she pulled on a fluffy old sweatshirt, panties, jeans and the pair of garish green-and-pink-striped slippers Kyle and Lena had picked out for her last Christmas. She suspected it was a tongue-in-cheek gesture on her sister's part, but Lena knew Abby would wear them because Kyle gave them to her. Of course her sister was right.

By the time she had finished all the necessities and had gotten down stairs, Kyle had set three places at the kitchen table. She smiled. Jesse always ate butter eggs with them.

She had so far put Kyle off when he asked when Jesse was coming home, and now she took the extra place setting and put it away in the cupboard.

"Kyle," she called and then noticed the back door was slightly ajar. He didn't usually play outside this early, but he didn't usually get up before seven o'clock.

She stepped outside to see her nephew standing on the top landing of the apartment stairs talking animatedly to Reed Maxwell. Reed looked as awake as Kyle was and he was nodding. After a moment Kyle turned and ran down the stairs and right up to where she stood in the doorway.

"Jesse's brother is comin' and eat butter eggs with us." Kyle's bright blue eyes shined in the morning light.

"You invited Mr. Maxwell?"

"Yeah. 'Cause you said he was taking Jesse's place."

She hunkered down in front of him.

"I said he was going to be staying in Jesse's place. I meant staying in Jesse's apartment, not taking Jesse's place."

Kyle looked stricken.

"But don't worry, sweetie."

She looked up at Reed as he stepped up onto her back porch.

"Good morning." They greeted each other as she stood.

Today he'd donned dark slacks, a navy blue golf shirt that stretched across the planes of his chest, and he had on his brown dress shoes again. His clothing showed off his body, made his eyes even darker and made her notice his hair glisten in the morning sun.

He looked tasty.

Jesse's brother was now about to eat at her table because she wouldn't be selfish and countermand Kyle's invitation. If he didn't want to eat with them, let him be the bad guy. Let the personality Jesse claimed he had come out into the open. It would make it a whole lot easier to send him away if he were a mean and angry man.

"Can he eat with us anyway?" Kyle asked, his eyes wide.

She cleared her throat before she spoke. "Of course he can eat with us."

She looked at Reed and raised her eyebrows in a silent question to see if eating with them was something he wanted to do.

"I can go to the diner," he said, addressing Abby.

"And you'd get a great breakfast. You'll get a great breakfast here, too, if you want to stay."

"It won't be too much trouble?"

"Not much if you like simple."

Kyle twisted back and forth between the

two of them, eagerly trying to untangle the adult speak in his five-year-old head.

"It's my favorite."

"And since Kyle already invited you, I can't very well turn you away." She smiled at each of them.

And then Kyle faced Reed. "You wanna eat with us, don't you?"

"If your aunt is sure it's all right," he said, and looked from Kyle to Abby.

She kept smiling. What the heck else could she do? "Jesse used to eat butter eggs with us. We'd be happy to have you join us."

"Then nothing in the world sounds better than butter eggs," he said, grinning down at Kyle. His perfect lips spread wide, white teeth in straight rows, his face shaved and smooth and crinkles at the corners of his eyes.

Sexy in the morning.

"Yippee." Kyle jumped up and down.

Uh-uh. Yippee, Abby thought, and when Reed looked up at her still grinning, the full force of his smile smacked her right between the eyes. "Oh, my."

"What?" Reed asked, his smile fading a little.

"Oh, well, it's just you, um, really look nice

when you smile like that." Shyness wasn't usually her thing, but the men in her life weren't usually stunningly gorgeous, ever, let alone first thing in the morning.

"Thanks. My grandmother used to tell me that."

"And you, um—here's a cliché—clean up nice," she finished, and sighed at her lack of grace under pressure. Not peak mental performance for a former trauma nurse.

He studied her attire, including her green-and-pink slippers. She wished she had put on a brassiere, but she had at least untangled her hair a bit.

"And you do casual breakfast attire rather nicely," he said after only a moment's thought.

She noticed her faded sweatshirt with only half a decal of a running grizzly bear remaining on the front of it.

"You are also so very polite, so early in the morning."

"Grandmother taught me that, too."

Was it her imagination or did his eyes just sparkle? She badly needed to get away before she drooled.

"Kyle, go in and get the eggs and butter

out. I'll be in soon." She turned to Reed. "I haven't started the eggs yet. You can come in or I can call you when things are ready."

"I could help. My kitchen skills are limited, but I can butter things really well."

"I bet you can."

Abby fled into the kitchen before she could say anything more to embarrass herself. Reed followed. What else could he do? He was polite after all and he had volunteered to help. Maybe she could pretend he was Jesse. Jesse would go play with Kyle while she cooked. Put this man with the boy? She wasn't sure that was such a good idea, either.

She grabbed the loaf of bread she had made the night before and the bread knife and turned intending to hand them to Reed. When she looked into his dark-lashed eyes, she knew why women in historical novels got all "vapory" when the hero gave them an unguarded smoking gaze.

Up close in her small kitchen, Reed Maxwell radiated heat. Caveats about he might be Kyle's uncle aside, he was all sexy muscle in that tidy rich-man way. And he smelled good, like a hot spicy afternoon in a mountain meadow.

If she hadn't been holding a loaf of bread and a knife, she might have spread her palms across his chest just to feel the power beneath that dark blue shirt. Drawn him close...

She blinked.

"Forgive me," she said and handed the bread and knife to him. Lifting her chin to indicate the breadboard on the counter behind him.

He turned away and she nearly fell over with relief. Reed Maxwell should go away. Far away. For all their sakes.

Oh, God. How was it possible for her to go so long without a man and suddenly her heart was leaping in her chest at the nearness of this one, Mr. There's No Way man?

"Can I break an egg?" Kyle pushed the high stool up to the counter and clamored on top.

"Yes, and tell you what. Every time you get all the egg in the bowl, you can break another." Abby handed Kyle the bowl and then she put a dollop of butter in the frying pan and turned the burner on low heat.

She glanced over her shoulder at Reed—once. Once was enough. One eyeful of flexing forearm muscles as he held the knife and sawed through the crispy crust of the bread had her gluing her attention to Kyle and the eggs breaking. She convinced herself she needed to watch carefully for shell fragments.

She had no idea how she was going to get through butter eggs and no idea how she got so attracted to a man who might be the enemy. Yes, she did. She knew herself well enough to realize she believed in the good and honesty of all people—until they proved otherwise. Believing had gotten her in trouble in the past and probably would again. So be it.

She could see herself raising a forkful of scrambled eggs to her lips and having them tumble into her lap as she gazed at the handsome man across the table.

Oh, she was in trouble.

REED LEFT THE APARTMENT above Abby's garage and headed this time to the town square park. The day was as beautiful as yesterday had been. He had a feeling, though, the tough winters made up for the glorious summers, otherwise these mountains would be as heavily populated as any southern state. The peace and quiet held a certain allure.

Breakfast had been great, as promised. Abby did eggs and butter so well, they melted in his mouth and if he forgot everything else in all their worlds, she and Kyle were a delight to spend time with.

Reed usually had breakfast alone at home or at the counter at the deli, or in his office. Sometimes he ate with a client or with his partner, Denny, when they were out of town together. He never thanked God for his food and he never laughed over toast, or listened to a child giggle about the antics of a hamster called Piglet.

Reed pulled up to the edge of the town square and found an open parking spot.

In the center of the square was a flagpole surrounded by a riot of flowers. Leading up to the pole from all corners of the park were walkways flanked by ornate, old-fashioned looking lampposts. In the center of one of the triangles created by the sidewalks was a stage with a newly built sheltering roof supported by stout six-by-six pieces of lumber. Picnic tables and park benches were scattered around in random places, one bench was occupied by a woman rocking a stroller and one of the tables by people playing checkers.

Two men sitting at a table in the shade of a group of large pine trees waved him over. When Reed approached, the men stood and introduced themselves. Clem worked at the post office and Harry at the feed store during the summer and taught juniors and seniors at the high school the rest of the year. On the table sat a carafe of coffee and a plate of doughnuts with dripping pale blue frosting.

Reed was going to need some serious gym work and soon, he thought as he sat down at the table, just in time to frighten away a chipmunk that tried to seize the day, or the doughnut, as the case might be.

"I had Jesse working for me for a few weeks unloading trucks and stacking shelves," Harry said. "He was a hard worker, but he was too skinny for that kind of stuff. Not enough heft to balance the bags. Now you, you could do the job."

Reed looked down at his jeans and open-collared shirt and back up at the man.

Clem was grinning big.

"I get it," Reed said. "Humor."

Both men laughed and then Clem got a serious look on his face.

"What?" The look made Reed uneasy.

"It's just that, well, was Jesse okay? I mean, was there something real bad in his past?"

Reed thought of Jesse's embarrassment of never inviting his friends over because of their mother's drunken antics. Then there was the time their father planned a weeklong trip for just the guys. Jesse was so looking forward to it, but when the day came, their father canceled without giving a reason. "What makes you ask?"

"Well, I'm not a shrink or anything like that, but as a teacher they school us to recognize such things in the kids. Jesse always seemed kind of sad." Harry looked uneasy as he spoke, as if there was more he wanted to say.

Birds chirped and the chipmunk scolded. The warm wind of the late morning felt clean and soothing, yet the look on Harry's face didn't reflect the effects of the wind. Clem munched a doughnut.

Reed leaned forward on his elbows, picked up Harry's gaze and held it. "If there is something I need to know about Jesse, tell me."

"I know it's been a while since you've seen your brother and that you've talked to a lot of people in town about him, but do you think he might do something to himself?"

"Hurt himself? Kill himself?"

"Hurt himself, more like." Harry looked a little relieved that Reed had caught on.

"Continue," Reed said.

"He didn't seem suicidal, more like reckless." Harry gestured for patience and understanding and Reed relaxed his body language. "Jesse was never reckless with anyone else or with anyone's things. He would go hiking alone and one time he practically crawled back to town. Now, there are plenty of people around here who like to hike. He could always find someone if he planned on a difficult one."

"And he—" this was Clem, who mostly sat nodding and eating doughnuts "—got sick once and didn't tell anybody, and Abby had to get the EMTs to carry him out of that apartment and into the clinic where they could treat him."

"I'd like to say I don't think he'd do anything too careless," Reed said, feeling the regret of not having kept closer with his brother, "but I haven't seen him in a few years and haven't heard anything from him in over a year."

"He's a tough nut to crack," Harry added.

Not if you knew his background, Reed thought.

"I'll let someone in town know if I hear anything from Jesse," Reed said as he pushed up from the table.

"It would be much appreciated if you did," Clem said as the two men stood.

Reed shook hands with the men and turned away. He had to ask himself what he was doing here, disrupting these people's lives. And trying to clean up his family's mess was probably not a good enough answer.

He stopped at Alice's Diner. If Abby was going to drive him out into the countryside, the least he could do was to bring lunch.

A half hour later, he pulled into the drive-way at Abby's place and a pickup truck pulled in behind him. Kyle leaped out of the truck and darted toward Abby, who waited for him on the porch. The truck left as quickly as it had arrived and Abby waved at the driver.

"I got candy." Kyle held up the colorful plastic bag of party junk and picked up his pace until he ran full speed at her. "Angus and I won some games and we got candy."

He thought of the Tootsie Pops on the kitchen table. He liked Kyle. Whether or not the boy was his flesh and blood, he liked him. He liked a kid. A first, he thought, in his entire adult life. What would be next?

ABBY HELD HER SQUIRMY nephew and scrunched him to her, wondering if she would ever feel as enthusiastic about anyone else.

"Can we go now? Can we go to Gramma's now?" he asked as he hugged back and then wiggled to get away.

"Run in and get the knapsack you packed this morning," she said, and let him go. "And save that candy for Grandma's house."

After Kyle ran into the house, she looked up and saw Reed standing beside his car. She smiled at the sight he made, arms crossed over his chest, strong lean legs spread in an open stance. There must be tongues wagging all over town about *that guy Abby's got staying over at her place*. That handsome guy in the fancy clothes.

Her next-door neighbors, Cora and Ethel, who ran the boardinghouse, were without a doubt peeking through the eyelet lace curtains at this very moment. Let them peek. They deserved a treat from time to time.

He reached into his car and brought out a paper bag.

"Thought I'd return the favor," he said as he walked toward the porch. "If you haven't eaten, that is."

The paper bag in Reed's hand had Abby licking her lips. "Is that from Alice's Diner?"

Kyle burst out of the door with his candy bag in one hand and a small backpack in the other. She had, at his insistence, let him pack his own things. She hoped he had at least one pair of clean underwear in there.

"Hi, Reed!" Kyle called as he ran past toward her small SUV parked on the other side of the rental car. The man had become "Reed" to Kyle over breakfast.

"I have to take Kyle to his grandmother's house and then we need to get started for the Harvey ranch."

Reed held his paper bag out to her and she took it and peeked into one of the cartons. "Is that Alice's chicken salad sandwiches?"

"The waitress assured me they would keep

a couple hours, in case you weren't home right away. Longer in the fridge, she said."

"Let's go, Aunt Abby," Kyle called from the window of her SUV.

"I'll be there in a minute, sweetie pie," she called to the child. "And put the candy inside your backpack."

To Reed she said, "If you bring the sandwiches, there is a picturesque place to eat them. You might as well see one of Montana's treasures." A beautiful treasure, a waterfall to be exact. A charming, little waterfall that always made her wistful. What the heck. She hadn't been wistful in days, maybe weeks. And maybe if she didn't drool on him, Reed Maxwell wouldn't know just how wistful she could get.

"Scenery with our food sounds good."

"There's a cooler with a cold pack and some bottles of water in it. Stow the sandwiches and let's go."

Five minutes later, when they arrived at her mother's house, Kyle freed himself from his booster seat, leaped out and raced toward his grandmother.

Delanna Fairbanks sauntered off the porch of her small yellow house and across the yard toward Abby's SUV. Her auburn hair with a few strands of gray flowed around her thin shoulders. She wore a pink rhinestone decorated T-shirt and on her long, shapely legs denim capri pants, clothing she no doubt found in Lena's closet.

Kyle flew into her arms and the two of them hugged and then danced around. Then hand in hand they walked to the car.

"Hi, Mom," Abby said.

Her mother wasn't looking at her, she was leaning in the driver's side window to stare at Reed. She stood up where only Abby could see her face and mouthed, "Wow!"

Abby mouthed "shut up" back, but gave her a grin. Sometimes her mother was just right and there was no use debating.

Reed climbed out and walked up to Delanna.

"Hi, I'm Reed Maxwell, Jesse's brother." He reached out for a handshake.

"I'm Delanna Fairbanks, and whatever Abby has said about me, take it with a grain of salt." Delanna took his hand in both of hers and squeezed as if she were welcoming him into the family.

"Can we go now, Gramma?" Kyle tugged

on his grandmother's leg until she let go of Reed's hand.

"Pleased to meet you, Reed."

He was grinning like a fool. Delanna did that to people. "I am pleased to meet you also, Delanna."

"Gramma."

Delanna took Kyle's hand and tweaked his cheek. "Let's go already."

The two of them ran toward the house. Her mom turned back for a moment and gave Abby a we'll-be-just-fine wave.

Then her mother leaned down and said something to Kyle who turned and called out. "Bye, Aunt Abby. Bye, Reed." He waved and turned as quickly away and plowed forward into the house dragging his grandmother with him. He didn't so much as hesitate. They would be all right.

Abby was proud of her mother. Delanna had stepped up and taken on some of the responsibility for her grandson, even before Lena left. It was almost as if having a child around made her mother finally grow up, something she hadn't done for her own children, but for which Abby had forgiven her and Lena would someday. Yes, Kyle and his "gramma" would be just fine.

Now if "Aunt Abby" would be all right...

When she turned away from the house, Reed had gotten back in the truck and was watching her. His dark eyes did the smoke thing. His hair did that glistening thing. And now she was the fool.

She was about to embark on a trip in a small SUV, a very small SUV, or so it seemed at that moment, and across a miniscule console sat the sexiest man she'd seen in a very long time, and the trip would take at least an hour's driving time there and another back.

And he did smell good.

She put her hands firmly on the wheel and pulled out into the street. She could do this. She could think of him in a professional manner, as if he were the relative of a patient. He was just another human being. The package he presented didn't mean any more than if he were old Mr. Hawes who'd come into the clinic for a physical last week—she wished.

She squeezed the steering wheel until her knuckles blanched.

"Is there something wrong, Abby?"

"Nothing's wrong." Abby relaxed her grip

on the steering wheel and let the blood flow back into her fingers. "In fact, things are peachy."

Or they will be peachy when Reed Maxwell had packed up his bags and left for the city. She chanced a glance at him and wasn't surprised to see his expression all but shouted his disbelief.

She gave a sharp laugh. "Fine. I'm just hoping Kyle and his grandmother don't burn down the entire village while I'm gone. Knowing them, it would please them both to have such a large bonfire for roasting wienies. It's kind of an immature leading the young with those two and I'm never quite sure who's who." Not even a lie, she thought as they passed the outskirts of the town of St. Adelbert and started upward into the mountains.

If she could just distract herself, maybe she could get through this trip. She took the clip from her hair and let the air from the open windows cool her skin.

The road rose quickly from the valley in which the town of St. Adelbert lay. The river that ran through town now tumbled over beige and gray rocks beside the road with the water reflecting the bright blue of the sky. Pine trees sandwiched the road and river for a while until the road climbed higher and then walls of rough stone rose on one or both sides of the SUV.

"Those little trickles of water coming out of the rock face—" Abby pointed out the window "—become ice cascades when the weather is cold enough."

"It's beautiful country."

Abby could hear the wonder in Reed's voice. Her own still held it, as she never got tired of the natural beauty.

"If we're lucky, we might see some of the wildlife."

"Lions, tigers and bears?"

"No tigers, I'm afraid, but we do mountain lions and bears, black and grizzly, quite nicely."

"*Nice* is not the word I might use if I encounter any of the above."

"Encounters are probably more rare than you think."

"They don't want to see us any more than we want to see them. I've heard, but do they realize how much I really don't want to see them?"

She laughed. "I'll see what I can do."

"What are these people like who live so far out in the country they might not know Jesse is missing?"

Reed spoke so formally, so un-Jesse-like.

"Well, Herman and Emma Harvey are old and they're razor sharp. They could probably survive anywhere, even in the city, but I still worry about them. They're too old to be living so far out by themselves." She smiled. "But I'm not sure anyone is even brave enough to broach the subject with them."

"What are the chances they'll have any information about Jesse?"

"I don't really know. But I do need to warn you about them."

He gave her a wary look. "Warn me?"

"These folk will either talk to you, tell you what they know, or they won't say more than a word or two. It depends on how Jesse left things with them, and more importantly, will depend on the impression you make on them."

She slowed to take a hairpin curve in the road as they climbed higher yet.

"Do I make a bad impression?"

She grinned. She couldn't help it. "The town is softening toward you. At first they were suspicious of what you wanted with their Jesse."

"Maybe I should have spread more cash around."

She knew he was kidding. "They'd have taken it, but it wouldn't have changed their minds. But hey, you've got me. The Harveys already like me. Besides, I brought them a bribe. Alice's Huckleberry Jam made lovingly by the owner of the town's diner."

"Jam?"

"Not just jam. Those berries grew in the wild, and out here you risk a bear encounter when you go out into the woods to pick them."

"Huh. Sounds tasty."

"You probably already had some. Alice sometimes uses it in the sweet rolls she makes."

"I might have had some of the bear jam—"

"Huckleberry."

"But I don't have anything against a good strawberry or even apricot jam. Not many bear encounters while harvesting those fruits I'd guess."

"You're such a city fella."

"I would be that." He smiled as though he enjoyed the truth.

He lost some of his uptightness when he smiled, and the smile might have drained some of the tension from her, too. She tried to see that as a good thing.

"Anyway, I called just before we left and told them we were stopping in to see them. They said they'd be happy to share a pitcher of lemonade with us."

"Since we're visiting in person, I assumed they didn't have a phone."

"They have a phone," she said, but didn't look at him.

"So this could have been done over the phone?"

"If you're trying not to sound annoyed, it's not working very well." She paused and when he didn't say anything, continued, "Did I say they were old? Make that very old, like two years older than dirt. I wasn't telling them anything like *Jesse's missing* over the phone."

"That seems reasonable. Although I'm used to having things move faster."

"There is fast here, but it's on a slightly

different trajectory, one you might not recognize."

He turned away to look out the window. "I didn't mean to sound insensitive."

She let that one go.

CHAPTER SIX

ABBY SEARCHED FOR ANOTHER topic and chose one she hoped might be more mundane. "What do you do for a living? Jesse was always sort of vague on that topic."

"It's a vague kind of business. My partner and I invest for businesses. Sometimes we buy other businesses, sometimes real estate. Whatever best suits a particular client's needs."

That information was more unsettling than she would have liked. She now knew for sure his money and influence were enough for him to get Kyle away from her while Lena was overseas. Her stomach clenched as it always did when she thought of her sister in a hostile zone. In the blink of an eye, if Kyle lost his mother, he could lose everything he ever knew: his mother, aunt, grandmother and his home. Abby prayed she would know the right thing to do if her nephew ever faced such a future.

Too complicated. Too scary to think about for very long.

In a perfect world, she'd just ask Reed what he thought about the possibility of Kyle being Jesse's and what they should do about it. In a dream world, he'd tell her it would be great to have a nephew and that the boy could come for a visit when he was older, about eighteen—and a half. In the meantime, he'd busy himself setting up a college fund.

That could be just what would happen. Maybe Reed Maxwell was a good man, a fine man. He could also want to take Kyle away. Did that make him bad? If it harmed Kyle, it might.

Heaven help her, she needed to make her mind go someplace else.

Think of him as a nice man. He hasn't done anything that should make her think anything less of him. And he did look nice with the dark knit of his shirt stretched across muscles that nearly begged to be touched. His face cleanly shaven did the same for kisses.

She couldn't let herself go there, either.

She concentrated on the whine of the

SUV's tires on the roadway, the tuneless hum of the wind rushing in the window. And then on the heat she imagined radiating from the man beside her.

The scenery. She drummed her fingers on the steering wheel and concentrated on the scenery. She loved the land of crags and scrub-covered hills with the soaring peaks visible between stands of tall pines.

She was about to round a curve that would showcase snowcapped peaks. When she did she watched Reed. His lips parted in awe and she smiled. He did appreciate some of the same things she did about the valley.

St. Adelbert had adopted her, twice, once as a young preteen along with her mother and sister, and not long ago when she needed a place to come home to. By the time she returned a second time, life had betrayed her and she was so fragile she had almost cracked, but the valley welcomed her as if she were whole and a good addition to the family of folk.

Thinking of her life in Denver reminded her of her friend Carrie, the creepface. It usually took the two of them at least a half-dozen messages between them before they finally got to talk. The first one in the chain of messages got to think up their nicknames for the chain. Creepface was on its fifth or sixth link in the current chain.

"I never imagined there was so much wilderness out here."

Reed's voice split the silence, and Abby gave a startled laugh.

"I don't know if the folks round here would much appreciate you callin' their spreads 'wilderness,'" she said, affecting her best cowpoke drawl. "We are just passing the Whispering Winds, where the doctors from the town's clinic live."

She pointed out the window on his side of the SUV and then to the land ahead of the truck. "And up ahead is the Shadow Range where the Doyle family lives. Mother, father, three sons and two of their wives."

"I met Baylor Doyle at the diner."

"He's the youngest unmarried son." She continued pointing as she spoke.

"Don't tell me he's the smallest."

"Ha ha. Anyway, that's where we're stopping on the way back to check up on Evvy." She pointed again. "And over that ridge is the Lazy D—"

He covered her hand with his and lowered her finger. "I get it. Nice—uh—farmland?"

She pulled her hand away. "Wilderness might be a better call on your part."

"Ranches," he offered instead.

She nodded. Though what she wanted to do was to rub away the feeling of his touch from the back of her hand. She'd missed the intimate touch of a man. Not that Reed's touch had been intimate, not really, not on his part, but to her it had been a caress.

"Yeah, ranches."

They rode in another long silence, until they came upon a familiar landmark.

"Frogs." It was his turn to point out the window as they approached the rock formation that looked like a couple of pond creatures hunkered down and ready to leap. "Somehow, I didn't expect them to be so—"

"Green?" She curled her lips in. "They used to be greener. Nature is helping by fading them. No one could ever prove it, but we always believed the Farmington brothers painted them a hideous bottle-green when they were teenagers."

Reed laughed. A nice sound. A sound that tickled her pulse, she admitted.

"I think they'd look more froglike," he said speculatively, "with a few spots, maybe they'd even look artsy."

"I'm afraid the Farmington brothers were more into mischief than realism or art."

Shortly after the frog rock formation, she turned the SUV down a narrower road. "It's rougher from now on. Be prepared for bouncing around a bit."

"I think I can handle it."

They had been gaining altitude for a while and now they dropped slowly down into another valley and the new silence between the two of them made her weary. He was Jesse's brother, she could be friendly to him. Maybe if she was, he'd think better of her and the valley his brother had chosen to call home for a short while. Maybe he'd even walk away without prying too deeply.

"What was Jesse like as a kid?" A reasonably neutral territory she hoped, as long as the subject of Kyle didn't come in tandem with Jesse. That was a place Abby didn't want to go—especially since she had nowhere to go with it. *Lena, when you get home…*

"He might still be one," Reed answered,

interrupting her Lena rant before she got it going well.

"A kid?"

"He never seemed to like playing the part of the grown-up."

"Yeah." Abby concurred. "His favorite place in Denver was the zoo, especially the lorikeet enclosure. He might still be feeding them as we speak if Lena and I hadn't dragged him out of the aviary. He had a T-shirt dyed lorikeet colors."

"Lorikeets are birds."

"Very brightly colored little birds. Popular in zoos because they will tamely eat nectar from a cup you hold for them."

Reed kept his gaze turned to the scenery. "Jesse used to climb trees to look in bird's nests. One day he brought a newly hatched robin in the house. He'd found it on the ground."

"Tough one. What happened to the bird?"

"As far as Jesse knew, it went to the local Audubon society to be raised and flew off to a long and satisfying bird life."

Abby wanted to backpedal and take back the conversation. She didn't want to see Reed Maxwell and his family as kind, thoughtful enough to spare a young Jesse's feelings. *Never mind,* she wanted to say, but instead said, "That was a nice thing to do for a kid."

"One of the nannies knew her life would be easier if Jesse didn't know."

"One of the nannies?"

"That's how Jesse and I were raised, mostly."

"Oh." Wow. She didn't know what to say to that, but apparently she didn't have to worry about feeling too guilty about not wanting to get to know the Maxwell family too well. If Kyle was Jesse's, the Maxwells might take him away only to be cared for by the hired help.

She couldn't let that happen to her sister's child.

"We weren't exactly dream children and Mother, well…" Reed continued.

Mothers might be a better conversation topic. "'Mother, well…' I know that one. There are a lot of 'wells' attached to my mother."

"For instance?"

She glanced over at him. He now sat turned toward her, the expression on his face inquisitive—on his handsome face, she corrected, a face she'd like to reach out and touch. She turned to concentrate on the rare straight stretch of road. "It's not a very interesting story. Trust me."

At least she wasn't interested in telling him. Delanna Fairbanks was not the open book she appeared to be. Abby knew her mother's carefree attitude hid a heart that ached for more love than two daughters and a grandchild could give her. Maybe Abby should agree to dinner with the undertakers.

How bad could it be?

Sometimes, when she wasn't behaving like a twentysomething, her mother was very wise. When things had first started to go wrong in Denver, her mother urged her to return to St. Adelbert, but Abby had resisted. She should have listened....

"Where did you go?" Reed asked.

"Um, what?"

"You went away for a while."

"Thinking, I guess."

"About your mother? I've had to think about mine a lot lately." He gently poked her arm with the tip of one finger. "Come on. Tell me. Make me feel better about mine."

Abby expelled a sharp breath. "She wants me to go on a double date with her."

"You don't like her company?"

"I like her just fine. She wants us to go out with the town undertakers, funeral directors, father and son."

"Undertaker isn't a hot enough field for you?"

She looked over to confirm he was kidding. "Thought I might have to boot you out for that comment and leave you walking back to Chicago."

"Hey, somebody has to be the funeral director. I'm always glad there are people out there who want to take up those kinds of professions."

"She's looking for husbands for us. Mother never had anyone to take care of her, ever. Her mother was apparently, ah, not there for her, and now she's searching before it's too late. But please—" she waved a dismissive hand "—let's not go down the undertaker road."

He shrugged away the undertakers. "My mother had legions to take care of her and she managed to live a rough life anyway."

"I'm sorry for her," she commented, glad to switch back to his mom.

"Please, don't be. She feels sorry enough for herself."

Abby scowled at him.

"Hey, I'm out west trying to find my brother so she can ask his forgiveness and make up for her neglectful past. That makes me not the worst son in the world."

"Maybe not the worst. Did you forgive her?"

"Thanks," he said and returned to studying the scenery. "And did I forgive her? I keep asking myself that question."

The conversation lapsed again. Mothers was apparently another conversation killer. That was probably good. Why she was talking to a hot guy about her mother and his...

Her mother might be right, she wasn't trying very hard to find a man. Although she wasn't dead to the benefits of having a good man around. Still, she had found a man—twice—and then discovered she was a bad seeker or at the very least, unlucky at locating a *good* man. Now she was going to get her life established, get Kyle safely into a home with his mother, and then she'd see about finding a man who wanted to fit into her life. Luckily, Chicago was a long way away from the St. Adelbert Valley and international corporate investment rarely entered into this remote region. Even her mom would have to admit Reed Maxwell, the trend-catching city man, and Abby Fairbanks, the small-town woman who just wanted peace in her life were a wrong match.

So, it couldn't hurt if her thoughts kept straying to such things as how muscled his chest was and how long and lean his legs were. When she realized she was white-knuckling the steering wheel again, she made herself relax and her mind think of something else, the scenery again. At least the forests and mountains were always there.

After another short while, she turned the SUV onto a dirt road and the bouncing began in earnest. "Yeehaa! Welcome to the back roads of Montana."

"Just like springtime in Chicago."

She laughed. "We'll see about that. I'm going to put the windows up."

"Why?" he asked as he pulled his arm inside.

"Wait for it."

He laughed and batted at the brown cloud that had managed to get in before she closed the windows.

"Welcome to one of the interesting facets of my world. Unpaved roads of dirt and rock."

"I'll take Chicago."

"I'm sure you would."

Abby drove fast enough to keep the brown cloud mostly behind them and every now and then jerked the wheel to the side to avoid a deep rut or a rock sticking up in the middle of the road. "Hang on, we'll be there soon."

Another turn and five rough minutes up a dirt lane, she pulled up in front of an old, two-story ranch house flanked on both sides by outbuildings with a barn behind the house.

"The Harvey ranch," she announced. "And the Harveys."

Emma and Herman sat in rockers on the porch with a pitcher of lemonade on a small table between them. Their tanned and lined faces held pleasant smiles. Emma's shirt was yellow-and-white-checked gingham and looked newly pressed. Herman's shirt was plaid flannel, faded. They both wore jeans, also faded. A rifle rested against the house a scant foot from Herman's elbow. Abby wondered what the man from the city would think about that.

"Do you suppose they've been sitting there waiting for us?" Reed asked.

"Yep."

"How long?"

"Considering there's still a lot of ice in the lemonade, not long." She turned halfway and spoke quietly. "Be very polite."

"I'll do my 'city fella' best."

REED SURVEYED THE PAIR, but stopped and held his ground to let Abby approach. She paused at the lower step of the porch where she stood straight and tall, confident. Whatever the Harveys might throw at her, she looked ready. "Hello, Emma, Herman."

The pair's smiles broadened in unison.

Abby handed the jam to Emma, who nodded and placed it on the table next to the lemonade tray. Abby turned back and gestured toward Reed. "This is Jesse's brother from Chicago, Reed Maxwell."

He smiled. It seemed a reliable choice.

"Welcome to both of you," Emma said.

As Abby stepped up onto the top step, the Harveys stood together.

Abby reached for Emma's hand. "Good to see you." She gave three solid shakes. Then she shook Herman's hand and smiled at each of them.

Reed stepped up and grasped Emma's hand firmly, surprised at how soft her skin was, but he was not surprised at how strong her grip was. He then gave the man a firm handshake. Herman wiped the palm of his hand on the leg of his overalls. Probably getting rid of the city fella cooties.

Abby turned toward him again, this time the glint of a smile lurking in her eyes.

Reed waited until Emma sat down and Abby had taken a seat in one of the rough-hewn timber chairs set out flanking the rockers. Positioned to divide and conquer if need be. His instinct was to lean on the porch rail and not sit at all, but he remembered Abby's warning. *If you act impatient with them, they'll shut you out.*

He was sure he didn't want to cross the Harveys on their territory. Especially since he might need the information they had—and they had a big gun.

"You drove a long way. What can we do for

you?" Emma's friendly tone let Reed relax
a little.

"My brother is missing."

They sat silently, each looking from Abby
to Reed and back again.

"Missing or just gone?" Herman asked in
a firm tone.

Reed hadn't thought there was much
distinction between *gone* and *missing,* but
when Herman's pale gray eyes nearly drilled
through him as he asked the question, he was
sure Herman did.

"Missing to me, but to Jesse, he might just
be gone."

"What do you want with him?" Emma
asked, her tone still soft.

"Our mother wants to see him."

"What do you want with him?" Herman
asked, still brusque.

"He's my brother. I'd like to see him, know
how he's doing. He hasn't written or called in
quite some time."

"He didn't talk about his family."

"He doesn't like us much."

"Why would we help you find him?"
Emma asked.

"Because he's my family, my brother, and

in the past, we survived for a long time by depending on each other." Reed knew as soon as he said those words the stakes rose. He and Jesse had survived as a team, and for the first time in his life he realized that without Jesse to feel responsible for, he would have turned out to be a different man. "I know he likes to do his own thing, but as much as he might not want to see me, I do want to see him."

The old ranchers looked at one another and then turned their gaze toward Abby.

Emma smiled at Abby and then the corners of the Herman's mouth turned up. The broad smiles deepened the lines in their faces, but didn't age them.

"That sounds like Jesse." Herman's eyes took on a bit more color. "He went 'missing' one day when he came to work for us. Walked off into the ranch. Showed up at sunset promising to come back the next day and do the work he was supposed to get done that day. And he did. Next time he came back, he cleared all the brush from around the house and set up a firebreak for us. We wouldn't be much use during a forest fire, so our best defense is to have the house as isolated as possible. He was a good worker when he took a mind to it."

"Sometimes a man like your brother is gone more than he's missing." Emma smiled and offered a glass of lemonade to Abby and then to Reed.

When everyone had a glass, they looked at Reed. He obligingly took a sip. Sour and maybe the worst lemonade he'd ever had in his life, and considering one nanny's penchant for the fake powdered stuff, he'd had some bad lemonade.

He held up the glass and the Harveys acknowledged him.

Abby sipped her lemonade and then spoke. "Jesse's been gone for almost two months, and I haven't heard from him. He said he planned to go to Utah, but he also said he'd be back soon, which usually meant a couple weeks. Did he by any chance talk to you about where in Utah he planned to go?"

Reed could tell from the tone of Abby's voice, she truly cared about what happened to his brother and he was thankful Jesse had such a friend. Then he found his gratitude toward her turning to something more as he watched, rapt, as she licked a drop of lemonade from her upper lip.

Herman leaned forward and Reed gave his attention to the man where it belonged.

"Well," Herman said. "He talked about wanting to be alone, to feel like he was the only person on the planet for a little while. Seemed like Escalante Wilderness area was maybe the place to send him."

"That's still a lot of land, right?" Reed couldn't help wondering if this was Jesse's final way to tell his family, maybe the whole world, he wanted nothing more to do with them.

"Two million acres of nowhere," Herman replied.

Reed looked at Abby. She tried not to show it, but he could tell she was stricken by the possibilities Herman had presented.

Mother, we may all be too late.

"In his own way, Jesse seemed like a respectful man, so he probably filled out a permit to go backpacking in there. The rangers might have some record of his coming and maybe going," Herman offered, as if trying to calm the direness of the situation.

"Maybe he didn't go there at all," Emma

said, her hand trembling as she poured the last of the lemonade into Abby's glass. "He could have gone anywhere. He might have some silly ideas, but he wasn't a fool."

Reed smiled his thanks. These might be the best compliments he'd ever heard anyone pay to his brother, respectful and not a fool. "You could be right. We might be jumping to conclusions."

As Abby drained the lemonade from her glass, Herman leaned back, took a pocket watch out and flipped it open. "We'll be saying a prayer or two for the young Jesse. Glad you folks could stop by and see us." Then he flipped the watch closed.

"Not so fast, Herman," Emma said, putting a hand on her husband's arm. "I have a couple of questions for these two."

Abby and Reed exchanged glances, then they focused on Emma.

"Will we be having a wedding in St. Adelbert?" Emma stared at Abby when she spoke.

Abby blushed. "Oh, Emma, Jimmy and I broke up while I was in Denver."

"I'm not talking about him, silly. I'm talking about the two of you."

"Us? Reed and I?" Abby blurted.

"I might be old and goin' on to blind, but I can still see the sparks flying between the two of you, and there's kind of a warm glow that flares out around you when you look at him." Emma nodded at Reed.

Abby looked at Emma and at Herman, but not at Reed and he was glad. He had no answer for her.

"Emma," Abby said, "I'm afraid Reed will be going back to Chicago soon."

"So?"

Abby shrugged and grinned. "So I'll just have to keep looking."

Emma laughed. "Well, I think the two of you should think about it anyway."

Reed took Abby's arm. "We will."

Abby turned, gave him a puzzled look and shook his hand loose from her arm.

"Good, then." Emma stood.

While everyone said goodbye, Herman hefted the lemonade tray and held it out for a moment while Reed and Abby deposited their empty glasses.

Emma picked up the jar of jam and nodded her thanks at Abby.

"Sorry if we weren't much help to you,"

Herman said. "But you might want to talk to that Fred fella in town. Jesse mentioned him a few times. I think they spent some time together after Jesse quit working at the auto shop."

"Thanks. I'll do that," Reed said. "And thanks for speaking with us."

The Harveys turned and went into the house, taking the lemonade pitcher, the jam and their big gun and closed the door behind them.

"I guess we're done," Reed said to the closed door and then turned to Abby.

She glanced at him, hurrying down the stairs.

"How do they manage out here by themselves?" Reed asked as he hurried after Abby and climbed into the SUV as she did.

"They sold their land to a guy who brings game hunters. But they kept the right to live there until they die, and once a week, Barry Farmington delivers supplies."

"The frog painter?"

"Poetic justice, hey?"

Reed nodded. "How does Jesse fit in with the Harveys?"

"Since Herman fell off the barn roof and

nearly died, they decided the best way to stay on the ranch was to have someone else do the dangerous stuff. And I suspect Jesse might have caught on to the positive energy that seems to surround them. It's the kind of thing he likes."

As Abby bounced the SUV back down the dirt lane to the road, Reed wondered if he'd ever find his brother or even if he ever really knew him.

"It's kind of scary to think of Jesse all alone out there by himself," Abby said. "I hope he's all right no matter where he is."

"Do you think he can handle Escalante or that place Herman mentioned?"

"He's pretty good at survival skills. He would go off with a pack of supplies and come out of the backcountry just fine two weeks later. He's got a chance."

"I hope you're right." Reed thought about his brother facing the wild country by himself and he couldn't help remembering the boy crying in his bed at night refusing comfort. "I'll call Monday about the permit at Escalante and see if they have anything."

ABBY NAVIGATED THE ROUGH roads back to the highway and then settled in for easier driving. Reed sat looking pensively out the window. She knew he was thinking of Jesse and found herself wanting to comfort him again. This time it wasn't just the nurse in her.

"It's hard not to worry about Jesse," she finally said. "But he gets mad when you do."

"That's true."

Abby had to grin. "But we do it anyway."

He smiled at her and no doubt about it, the spark Emma talked about fired between them.

They rode in silence for a while until Abby asked, "Are you hungry?"

Reed looked over at her and smiled again. "I have been since I bought the sandwiches."

He did look so good when he smiled—and that might not be "so good."

She studied the road. It was so much safer.

"Do you have to get to your patient soon?"

"Just to the Doyle ranch this afternoon. Evvy's doing fine she claims, but I'd like to see for myself. Anyway, I have a place in mind, the one I mentioned earlier, that would make a great spot to—" she was going to say, have a picnic, but she wasn't sure she wanted to feel that comfortable with Reed Maxwell "—see a bit of Montana scenery while we eat, if you're interested."

"It is beautiful out here."

"Out here being west of the great flatlands, away from civilization?" she asked.

"I'm a flatlander? Is that a bad thing?"

"Wrap your head around this one. Many of us think you people are as deprived as you think us mountain folk are, so far away from the big cities. The only thing I feel deprived of out here is cell phone towers and I don't feel deprived of them all that often."

"What do you like about living here?"

"Denver was too noisy and St. Adelbert is like having a very large family."

"Maybe I should move my mother here. Then she'd have all the family she'd need."

"Hmm. Your mother and mine could be friends. You'd have to stay here, too."

"Why?"

"Because—" *if you were all here I'd never lose Kyle* "—I won't be responsible for anyone else's mother. Mine's enough."

"I guess Mother will have to make do in Chicago."

"Too bad. I had a feeling you might be falling for the charms of the mountains, and being gossiped about, of course," Abby said as she turned the SUV into a small pullout.

"The gossip's just more overt here." He grinned at her as she stopped. "At least here, it's easier to find out what they're saying about you."

She sat for a moment taking in the warmth of his smile. He really didn't seem to mind the people's penchant for living in your pocket. Many outsiders found it hard to take. "We'll need to hike a little way, if that's all right."

"I'm getting used to the altitude. I think I can hack it."

Abby tucked water bottles in the holders of a waist pack that was filled with supplies. Reed took charge of the sandwiches and they started up the trail lined with wildflowers and buzzing bees. The sun shined down from a brilliantly blue sky and small white clouds floated above the mountaintops.

"It smells good," Reed said quietly from behind her.

"Wildflowers and lack of pollution."

"Very unlike the streets of Chicago."

Every step she took up the rocky trail,

Abby could feel Reed Maxwell's presence behind her. Before she could even hear the sound of the waterfall, her body was humming with unwanted energy and she wondered if she should turn back to the car and get them back to town.

At a fork in the trail, Abby stopped abruptly.

Reed put a hand on her shoulder and she inhaled sharply from the startled sensation of wanting to turn around and, enemy or not, step into his arms.

CHAPTER SEVEN

"THE SHORTEST WAY IS that way." Abby pointed up a steep, rocky incline and resisted the urge to put her lips to the fingers resting on her shoulder. "But with your Chicago shoes, we should take the longer way."

"I can probably make it up that."

We'll see, she thought as she started up the incline.

She gave some of her attention to the trail ahead. With her hiking shoes on, it wasn't a difficult climb, but she had never gone up with a sexy man on her heels—or one in street shoes. She couldn't afford to slip and fall after giving him a hard time about his footwear.

"Thanks for thinking of me."

She quickened her pace. "Actually, I was thinking of how much I'm going to enjoy the sandwiches. If you hurt yourself, I might have to go hungry."

His laughter followed her up and so did he.

As she climbed, Abby realized how much she missed adult fun. Climbing at a thigh screaming pace the air seemed fresher. The wildflowers and pine trees seemed more fragrant when her mind didn't have to keep the needs of a child constantly in mind. She enjoyed the adults she worked with at the clinic, but that was work. Almost every waking moment outside the clinic involved a five-year-old, sometimes two or three of them. Right now she even enjoyed her lungs' demand for more air as she pushed up the trail. Hiking these days was usually at a short-legged little boy's pace.

She heaved her weight up one last large step onto the flat rock that led to the falls overlook. Then she let the breeze cool her off as she sauntered on slightly jittery legs to the edge and looked down into the tumbling water.

The sun streaked through the pine trees and created a rippling rainbow in the mist at the base of the falls.

"It's beautiful." Reed spoke from so close behind her, she thought she felt his breath on the shell of her ear. She would need only lean back a little and she'd feel the hardness of his chest against her back. It would feel so good to lean against someone again.

She sidestepped to dodge the emotion and sat down on the rocks overlooking the falls.

"I guess your city shoes didn't slow you down much."

"They might have, but my ego is too big to let me get too far behind."

He stepped over to the edge so he could see the falls looking, she thought, no worse for the wear except for splotches of brown dust on the legs of his black pants. In fact, the dust on his shoes, the pink cast to his cheeks, and what the wind did to his dark hair made him look less the city man. More attractive.

Someone she might want to…

"Sometimes," she said as she purposefully turned her gaze to the falls and her mind away from what she might want from him, "in the spring, there is so much water going over the falls it almost seems as though you can reach out and touch the rainbows."

"You more than like it out here, I mean, in Montana."

She gave a short laugh. The mountains fed her soul. How does one explain that sort of thing to a city person? "I do. It's not just the beauty and vast amount of peace and quiet. The mountains and the wildflowers, well, they never, um—"

"Judge you?"

Maybe he could understand. "Yes. The smell, the sound, even the textures and colors of the rock, trees, peaks and valleys soothe my brain, help me keep things in perspective."

The bright sun made her squint, and when he turned toward her the shadows deepened the dark of his eyes until she saw the mystery living there, along with the sexy. She wondered if she'd ever find out what that was all about.

She huffed out a breath of frustration that her mind, so used to being disciplined, now meandered like a lost soul down a path in a foreboding forest.

"I'm starved." She stuck her hand out for the bag he held. If she couldn't let herself lust, she could at least eat.

He sat down on the rock a couple feet away from her, and she handed him one of the boxed sandwiches, but when she took out the second sandwich for herself, the bag wasn't empty. She looked at him and then into the bag and back at him. "Oh, you are bad."

"Me? Bad? I didn't think you'd figure it out so soon. What gave me away?"

She pulled her hand from the bag and held up the pair of cookies wrapped in plastic wrap. "Not just cookies—the big ones and the best ones. Oatmeal chocolate chip with walnuts."

"Ah, good bad."

She nodded. Adult company. Hiking. Cookies. A warm sunny summer day. A sexy man. Did things get any better than this?

She looked at Reed Maxwell, really looked at him. The wind ruffled his hair and the smile lines around his mouth gave him an air of experience with laughter. When his gaze didn't waver from hers she realized they were staring. Man and woman sizing each other up. Wondering what men and women wondered when they took the measure of each other.

"I guess eating would be in order," she said, when she once again took control of her gaze and brought it to bear on the sandwich box in her lap. Hungry. She was hungry. A sudden image of what Reed might look like without the dark blue shirt flitted into her mind.

She snapped open the box and reached in for half the sandwich. By the time she brought it to her mouth she no longer knew what the drool was for, the man or the food. It didn't matter. The sandwich was all it was going to get.

"Good sandwich," Reed said after they had sat for several minutes eating in silence.

"We're spoiled. Alice, actually her name is Sarah, who owns Alice's Diner took over for her aunt, who wasn't Alice, either. Apparently Alice died several decades ago, and everybody just calls the owner Alice. Anyway the diner has always had good food. Tourists are often surprised. I think they expect greasy spoon fair or that people in Montana don't know anything about popular cuisine."

"Your Alice would do well in Chicago."

"Well, you can't have her. She came here to get away from the big city. Phoenix, I think."

"What about you?"

"What about me?"

"You came here to get away from the big city."

"Something like that. St. Adelbert is a great place to bring up a child, a safe place."

"How long have your sister and my brother known each other?"

Whoa. Not good. The question sounded innocent enough, but she sneaked a sideways look at him to try to tell if he was trying to accuse her of something. She knew the answer to his question, but having him ask after she had mentioned the "child," she knew she had made a tactical error. Six or seven years. Evade? Lie? Give it all away?

"Several years. They met after Jesse had been living in Denver for a while. He said he hated Chicago, but the easy escape to the mountains made Denver an okay big city." All vague. All the truth as she knew it to be. She took a bite of the second half of her sandwich, more for something to do as her hunger faded rapidly with the first half.

"He hated the family pressure in Chicago. As long as he was living in the area, he was expected to work for the family business. Our father could never stop bringing up how disappointed he was that Jesse wasn't holding up his end. Eventually, Jesse just stopped coming around to listen and then he moved away without telling us where he was going or even that he was leaving."

She could feel the pain in his voice, a missing brother, family, childhood memories. She wanted to blurt out everything she knew, well, everything she suspected, but would that help or hurt? All she knew for sure was the child was her sister's. Abby had held Lena's hand and empathetically felt every labor and delivery pain when Kyle was born. And she had taken care of Kyle for every day of his life since then, until today. The first day she had relinquished control for longer than the length of a workday. Now if she could just keep from stumbling her way into losing all control. "I don't think he told Lena about his family, about you, until they had known each other for a while."

He stared into the water falling over the uneven rocky surface. "Jesse does a good job of living under the radar. We only found out he was in Denver because our father plays golf with a banker who could tell him where Jesse's money had gone."

"That doesn't sound legal."

After a short bark of laughter he said, "I'm

sure the two of them found a way to justify what they were doing."

"I hope he's okay."

"My brother has somehow always managed to be okay, no matter what the world has thrown at him."

"He can charm the noise off a rattler. That's what one of the women neighbors says about him." She thought of Jesse's goofy grin, his lanky frame, his whatever attitude. "I hope it's enough."

Reed moved closer to her and put his arm around her shoulder. She held her breath, not knowing what to do, how to respond to the gesture.

"Thanks for caring about my brother," he said and gave her shoulder a soft squeeze. "He hasn't had that many people in his life who did."

She looked into his eyes and tried to see what was there. If it was up to her, missing brother or not, she'd lean in closer and kiss him on his sexy mouth.

"You're welcome." She jumped up and stepped away. "Um, there's a view you should see since we're here. It's only a little farther up the trail, if you're interested."

He stood and gathered the leavings of their lunch including the unopened cookies. "Lead on."

Abby hiked as fast as she dared. What she wanted to do was to hike as fast as she could and keep hiking. While hurrying over the uneven and sometimes steep terrain it was easier not to think of the man behind her, but she couldn't drag him through the whole mountain range hoping he'd give up and go home to Illinois.

They hiked over the next rise and the next. Eventually they reached a lookout. The land spread out in the deep frothy green of pine trees. On the far side, craggy mountains stood, silhouetted against the stark blue of the Montana sky.

"Pinus ponderosa. That's what the trees out there are," she said as Reed came up behind her and stopped on the rock outcropping. "The Montana state tree."

"Ponderosa pine?"

"One of its many names. The West was practically built on that tree. Railroads, buildings, bridges, just about everything of any size that was built out here was built using this tree." She could feel the heat radiating off his body so close behind her. Talk trees, mountains, anything to keep your mind occupied, she told herself as she casually took a step away. It might have been a mistake to trust herself to bring him here.

"I guess I never thought much about trees. Cattle, horses, pioneers, covered wagons, but it makes sense. They needed something to use to build things."

It was all so beautiful out here away from civilization. So private she and Reed could do anything here and the world would never know.

"Abby?"

Abby pretended she didn't hear him.

"Did you know there are sparks flying between us?"

Know it? She could feel them. The heat was trying to scorch her.

She turned slowly toward him and met his gaze and maybe she leaned forward a little, she wasn't sure. Reed reached for her and pulled her to him. When he lowered his mouth to hers, the kiss was soft and exploring and she leaned against his hard body and took in all the pleasure he was offering.

He lifted his mouth from hers. She supposed to let her flee if she was thinking of getting away.

"I have wanted to do that since you answered the door and became the most beautiful thing I'd seen in Montana."

She started to laugh. "You've got to be kidding." Although a part of her most definitely wanted what he said to be true. Beautiful.

He leaned in and kissed her again. This time he deepened the kiss and brought his arms around her as if she wasn't engulfed enough. She returned his kiss with an eagerness of her own. Kissing him was better than she'd imagined, far better.

She reached around behind him and ran her hands up and down his perfect back. Pleasure rushed wildly inside her until it began to seep into the tiny dark places where she held herself protected. Barriers began to fall. Inhibitions forced on her by her life began to crumble.

She pushed away. "It's been a long time since I've kissed a man and I'm not sure I've ever been kissed that well before."

A delicious smile curved his lips, but he didn't let her go. "It just seemed like the right thing to do. Emma's advice, you know."

"Wrong in so many ways, but thanks. I enjoyed it." She reached up and pressed her lips briefly to his. "However…"

"However?"

"Yes, *however*. I do have to get to the Doyle ranch to check on Evvy before they send out a search party."

"Would they do that?"

"They would. If I went missing, all able bodies in the town of St. Adelbert would come out looking."

"So you're that important?"

She knew he was teasing and smiled. "You've met many of them by now. What do you think would happen if one of us went missing? They'd be out searching for Jesse if they thought he was missing around here."

"Off to Evvy's it is." He dropped his arms to his side and stepped back so she could lead the way back down.

She started, careful to go fast enough that she had to concentrate on staying upright on the trail and not think too much about the man behind her. Kissing the man behind her. Liking the kiss. Wanting more.

REED GLANCED OVER AT ABBY as she smoothly maneuvered her SUV around another sharp curve. The ride back toward the Doyle ranch was taking place mostly in silence. But there wasn't much to say that didn't involve excuses for the kiss, for which there were none.

In the past, when someone said "I don't know what came over me" Reed knew he would have scoffed at the lack of logic, but now it felt like a stupid mind trick that might have some basis in reality.

Or not.

He did know what had come over him when he kissed Abby. She had. She was kind, generous and real and all those things made her as alluring as any glitzed-up city woman—maybe more. Best of all, he realized with a kind of tantalizing pleasure, she didn't want anything from him. In fact, she had made it pretty clear she didn't want big-city life, no matter what frills came with it.

He stared out at the scenery and after a while confessed that he was captivated by the package, the woman and her Western milieu.

It had to be the novelty.

It was easy to see the wealth here lived in the land and, not to be too corny, in the people. There were occasional transplanted Hollywood stars and cowboy wannabe corporate moguls hidden among the peaks, but for the most part, the people here were much closer to the battle for survival, closer to real life. The Harveys' need for a firebreak. The small business owners like John Miller at the hardware store and Taylors' Drug Store, even grizzly Fred. There was even a local furniture maker who cut down trees to make tables and chairs. There were no corporate layers between these people and life.

He wondered what it would be like to live where the mountains soared and valleys grew deep with Ponderosa pines and were spotted with ranches. He wondered what it would be like to live where you impacted people's lives and not just their overstuffed bank accounts.

He suddenly felt humble knowing there was a BMW in the garage of his downtown Chicago condo and his boat lay moored in the nearby marina, a rarely used boat that could probably pay for Abby's house and the taxes on it for the rest of her life.

He wondered if he could some how do that for her.

He quickly saw a few of the ramifications of that particular thought. Probably not a good idea. The best thing he could do for these honest people was to get what information from them he could about his brother and leave. Meddling with other people's lives was his mother's obsession, and he was sure the people here wouldn't like it any more than he did.

He would drive down to Utah and check with the park people to see if his brother had filled out a permit. If Jesse had done that, at least, Reed would know he had truly gone hiking in Escalante and when. If he found Jesse had been there, he could check with people in the nearest towns, if there were any, and see if they could shine some light on Jesse's whereabouts. If not, his only choice would be to fly back to Chicago and break the news to their mother, break her newly awakened heart most likely.

Abby turned the SUV into the relatively smooth gravel lane of what she had earlier pointed out as the Doyle ranch.

After a short drive, she pulled up in front of the house and stopped.

ABBY ADDRESSED REED, "I'll be about a half hour. You can stay in the truck, but Evvy Doyle will probably take offense and thus send one of her sons out here to fetch you." She grinned at him. "They're usually not armed, but it would be easier if you came in and had a cup of coffee while you waited. I promise it will be much better than the lemonade."

"I guess I'd like a cup of coffee," he said and pushed open the door on his side of the vehicle.

"Abby Fairbanks, you beautiful thing. How the heck are you?"

Abby climbed out of her truck. "Baylor Doyle, you handsome devil, I'm just perfect."

"I'll say so." He kissed her on the cheek and when she opened the back to get her bag of supplies, Baylor, big, blond and flirtatious, reached in and nabbed it before she could.

Reed got out of the SUV and came around back. Abby introduced the men and the two of them danced around each other like peacocks showing off for the hen, though they would deny it if she pointed it out.

Men. How she loved having them around.

"Baylor, is your mother still trying to set you up with Nan Hunter?"

"Nan and I are engaged."

"What?"

"Gotcha."

"Nan is nice people, Baylor. She shouldn't be saddled with a hopeless flirt."

"She's marrying some guy from Franksville."

"Baylor, take Reed in and give him a cup of coffee while I go see your mother."

"Sure thing, Abby. You want him back again or should I lose him in the back forty?"

Abby gave Reed a long contemplative look. "I think I'll have him back. He's got a mother, too, ya know."

She made a face at the two of them and headed off to see Evvy. Let's see how the city man survived under the scrutiny of a Montana rancher with his guard up. She and Baylor had been friends since junior high when two boys had tried to take advantage of a slight young girl with a mop of dark curly hair and Baylor took the affront personally.

After that, every kid in the school treated Abby with respect or they gave her space.

When she returned to St. Adelbert, Baylor had been first in line after her mother to welcome her home.

It was people like Baylor who made the valley a little piece of heaven she never wanted to leave.

"THAT WAS A FRIENDLY FAMILY, even the big guy in his own way," Reed said when they were back in the SUV and headed toward town.

"Our mothers used to try to get Baylor and I together, but we could never manage to see more than friendship in each other."

"He's very friendly."

Abby glanced at Reed and smiled. "He is. If he were a teddy bear, he'd sleep at the foot of my bed at night."

Reed gave her an odd look.

"Hey, I never kissed him at the waterfall," she said as she studied the road ahead.

"We had left the falls by then."

This time when she glanced at him she could have sworn there was heat in his eyes and she quickly shifted away. Abby wondered if she should ask Reed to come into her house and they could talk some more about what had happened between them at the falls. But then maybe she was making it up in her head that there was something to discuss. He was a big-city fella, a very good-looking big-city fella. Probably kissed women all the time.

"Here, have a cookie," she offered.

"Don't mind if I do."

At least she had accomplished her patient-care goals for the trip. The visit at the Doyle ranch had gone well. Evvy had learned to use her crutches the way she was supposed to. Not that she needed to lift a hand. Both her daughter-in-laws were at her beck and call, and from what Abby could tell, they all loved the arrangement.

She often thought it would be fun to be a part of an extended family like that. All three sons still lived at and helped run the ranch and two of them had wives and children.

The idea made her wistful until an image of the town funeral directors in wedding tuxes popped into her head.

She pushed the thought of the pair away and was rewarded with the memory of kissing Reed.

City man kisses Big Sky woman. He probably wanted to try something different, sample the Western fare. She couldn't fault him for that. She might have felt the same way about sampling what the city had to offer. The first kiss had been sweet and soft, the second demanding and made her insides feel warm and her knees soften to jelly. And when the feelings started all over as if was happening again, she jerked her mind away.

Maybe the young undertaker kissed like that.

Yeah, he kissed like that and nobody had snapped him up? Unlikely.

After more silence, she pulled the SUV into the driveway at her house and turned off the engine. *Run into the house and bolt the door* was her first thought, but didn't have a bolt on the door and maybe she'd give him a chance in case he wanted to talk.

"I was wondering—"

His cell phone burped a strange sound and he reached for his pocket to silence it. Although he had ignored two earlier calls with the same ring tone, his face was apologetic this time. "Excuse me. I do need to take this call. Thanks for taking me to meet the Harveys. I'll come down later." He waved as he raised the phone to his ear and leaped from the SUV.

In case he wanted to talk. What in the world had she been thinking? Give a man a chance to talk or run. Ha! Her experience said run was the popular choice among men, the only choice for one man—her father. She couldn't help but think he had run because of her.

She gathered the trash from their lunch and got out. It was just as well Reed hadn't lingered. His living above her garage had been enough to start tongues wagging. Their disappearing for several hours together wouldn't have helped.

The wagging shouldn't bother her, but it was important to be respected in town. Respect was part of what helped her feel she was a good fit for St. Adelbert. She was, after all, one of the few nurses in town, a person to be depended on in life-and-death situations.

She let herself in her back door.

Now after what the pair at the ranch had said about Jesse going to the most untamed part of Utah, Reed would likely feel the need to move on and the tongue-wagging would quickly find something more interesting.

The giddy memory of the feeling as he lowered his lips to hers filled her and she reveled in the delicious sensations.

Yup. Reed Maxwell needed to go.

Her landline phone started ringing as she pitched the trash in the can. She snagged the portable handset on the way to the bathroom to wash her hands and face. The minimal dust relief would have to do for a while until she had the time for more.

"Hey, how's the boonies, creepface?"

"Hi, Carrie," Abby said into the phone pinched between her ear and her shoulder. "The boonies are great. How are things in the big, dirty, vice-filled rat's nest of a city?"

Her friend, who still lived in Denver, laughed. "Hey, don't bad-mouth my city! Yes, there are more rats, more vices than you can shake a dirty stick at, but I kind of like some of them."

It was Abby's turn to laugh. "You would."

"Anyway, I only have a minute. We're expecting an ambulance to arrive soon, but I wanted to let you know...hang on." Carrie muted her phone and there was a sudden silence.

Carrie was a good nurse and they had been

good friends. In fact, Carrie was the only one who had openly taken Abby's side when she was accused of making a drug error that nearly killed an older woman.

"I'm back, but the ambulance is almost here. I just wanted to let you know someone was here asking about you."

"About me? Who? When?"

"Yeah, you. Just after lunch today. I only got the chance to call you now. Busy, busy, you know."

"Who was it, Carrie?"

"He said he was a private investigator."

Abby got a distinct sinking feeling. "What did he want?"

"I'm not sure. He wouldn't tell me why he was asking questions any more than I'd give him answers. He didn't know I saw, but he got a call from a 312 area code while he was here, and it seemed like it was from the person who hired him. Oops, I was going to look that up for you before I called. I didn't do that, either. Might be something related to the case and not really you personally, but I thought you would like to know."

"I did want to know, thanks." A sudden thought struck her. What if it had something to do with her sister or Kyle? "He didn't ask about Lena, did he?"

"He just asked about you. He wanted to know why you left Denver and if there might be anything about you that, he said, 'seemed off.' Weird, huh? Anyway, all I told him was he'd be lucky to have you as a nurse if he ever got caught snooping in the wrong place. He laughed, but I could tell he didn't think it was too funny."

Why would anyone be asking about her? The lawsuit was settled. Was he really a reporter? Did he suspect more dirt? "Thanks, Carrie. Say, you haven't heard anything about Jesse Maxwell have you?"

"Not a peep. I checked in with his old roommates like you asked me and they've heard nada. I hope he turns up soon."

A loud squawk sounded over the phone. The ambulance had arrived on Carrie's end.

"I gotta go. Give Lena a 'hey' for me." The phone went silent and Abby knew her friend was gone for good this time.

A private investigator, not looking for her, but looking into her past. She prayed there wasn't anything new going on.

She booted her computer up and went to get a glass of water. She sat down and slugged the water down as her online service worked on coming up.

While she waited, she read her mail, mostly bills, and wondered how her mother and Kyle were faring. Just fine, probably. People all over the world got along *just fine* without her constant oversight, and Kyle and her mother were probably among them. Now, if she could relax and let those two peas in a pod have a good time.

When her browser finally loaded, she typed in *Area code 312* and waited some more.

It did not take long before one word blasted her in the face like the punch from a combative patient. *Chicago.*

CHAPTER EIGHT

ABBY KNELT BESIDE THE bucket on her kitchen floor, scrubbing at the dirt that used to be there. She thought of the man in the apartment over her garage, of how his kisses made her brain scramble and the rest of her want more.

Area code 312. She scrubbed harder. Thinking of Reed was not why she was scrubbing the kitchen floor. She was scrubbing the kitchen floor because he had sicced a private investigator on her. It had to be him, and there were only two reasons why he would do that. Jesse and Kyle.

He wanted to see if she had anything in her background that would cast suspicion in her direction about Jesse's disappearance. She used the edge of her short fingernail to pry up a piece of stubborn something she had missed the first time she went over that area of the floor. Or he wanted to confirm his suspicions that Kyle was Jesse's son.

She sat back on her heels and tossed the sponge into the bucket. Scrubbing the floor was supposed to get rid of all thoughts of indictments against her...and of warm lips kissing her, and the hunger rising swiftly at the touch of those lips and rising even now.

She nabbed the sponge again and squeezed out the water. The water that splashed up onto the side of the yellow bucket was barely dirty after the second scrubbing. She pushed up and carried the pail to the sink.

If only she could get rid of the dirt in her past so easily, sponge out the false accusations, the lawsuit, the losing her job in disgrace, the reporters dogging her every move and helping to teach her the fear that still occasionally tried to consume her.

She rinsed the bucket and wrung out the sponge for the last time. That was the past. There was nothing she could do about it now.

Out the window behind the sink she could see the garage apartment and inside the apartment she could see Reed toweling his hair. His chest was naked and catching the late-afternoon light. Even from this distance, she could see his well-formed muscles flexing and relaxing.

Naked. For all she knew, he was naked all the way down to his toes.

She snapped her gaze down at the sink and tried hard to squelch the feelings racing through her at the thought of a totally naked Reed Maxwell, gleaming and flexing. Oh.

She got out a clean sponge and began wiping the cabinets over the counter, wiping away things like fingerprints and jelly globs, like the past, like kisses and wanting a man who could handle the world.

By the time she had finished cleaning the upper cabinet doors inside and out, she was satisfied she could forget the things she needed to forget.

When she sat at the kitchen table to sip the tea she had made an hour ago, her head filled with thoughts of what it might be like to have a man like Reed at her side.

Oh, dear, what the heck else needed cleaning?

Twilight filled the sky by the time she had finished the lower cabinets.

Reed Maxwell had to go, her brain said.

Her heart agreed. If they explored what had seemed to spark between them on the mountain trail, Kyle could pay the price.

Time to check on Lena again. She got up and rinsed the mug—she never had a sip of the tea—then started down the hallway toward the computer/storage room.

Maybe a short fling with Reed...

As she passed the mirror in the hallway, she murmured, "Stop that," under her breath.

Her online service came up quickly and she said a brief thanks for the strong signal. When her email popped up she scanned quickly for LenaFSOTW—Lena Fairbanks, Savior of the World.

Nothing from Lena. Not surprising. They often went out into the field, sometimes without any announcement and stayed out of contact for a couple of weeks. It had been almost that long since she had heard from Lena. Almost time to fulfill one of her responsibilities—to worry and pray harder for her sister's safety.

A subject line caught her attention on the second scan of her incoming emails. "About Lena" it said. Abby didn't recognize the sender, but didn't even consider sending it to the spam folder.

When she opened the email she quickly realized it was from someone in Lena's unit.

...they were supposed to be back three days ago. Heavy fighting broke out where her squad was headed and it could be a matter of cleaning up the place and getting back here when they're done.

I don't want to worry you, but Lena made me promise to email you if she didn't come back by today. She said you deserved to hear from a friend and, well, not from those solemn uniforms that might make a visit, or worse a phone call.

She said to tell you she loves you.

The message was signed by another woman soldier.

Abby sat back in her chair. The inferences in the email said Lena had expected this assignment to be quick and dangerous. She'd either be back soon or they would have run into danger—more danger than usual.

Please, please, please be okay, Lena.

Abby sent off a quick response that included a message of gratitude and a wish of safety for the sender of the email. Then she pressed the computer's off button and rolled the chair back. Tears filled her eyes and she blinked them away. There was nothing to cry about. Lena was fine and she was coming home for a visit as scheduled in a few months.

She sniffed and pushed up from the chair. What she really needed now was a bath and some sleep.

THE NEXT MORNING ABBY was just emerging from another fruitless check on Lena when the doorbell above her head jangled loudly, unexpectedly, scaring her half to death. It had to be Kyle and her mother. She brushed at the tears still in her eyes. Maybe they wanted breakfast. Maybe her mother had figured how bad a packer Kyle was and they came for his clean underwear.

She missed Kyle a lot and she was never so relieved at the thought of seeing friendly faces.

As she approached the front door, a figure, taller than her mother, cast a shadow through the curtain. She didn't know why Reed had come to the front door, and *he* wasn't a friendly face. She yanked open the door, prepared on all fronts to send him away quickly.

On the porch stood Sheriff Potts with his hat in his hand, his squad car parked in the street. Bad news.

Choking panic flashed up. She didn't let it capture her this time, but the tears she hadn't completely banished earlier burst forth in a flood.

"Abby?"

"Come in, Sheriff." She held the door open and stepped away so he could enter.

After she closed the door, she tried to look at him, but she only cried harder.

"I'm sorry. I'm sorry. I'll be right back," she said and pointed him into the living room before she took off for the powder room at the back of the house.

Several minutes later and somewhat composed, she entered the living room where the sheriff stood with his hat still in his hands. In his early fifties, he was graying at the temples, but had a body as strong as a mountain bear, now that he took better care of himself.

"I can come back later if this is a bad time." The sheriff stood stock-still as he made the offer. The people of the valley loved this law enforcement officer for his straightforward-ness and his integrity.

"No. Whatever it is you came to tell me probably needs to be told."

She motioned for him to sit on the couch and she took a chair nearby, clutching the fistful of tissues she had brought with her.

"Well, okay, if you're sure."

"Yes. I'm sure. I'm so sorry, Sheriff. I didn't mean to blubber at you."

He nodded. "We just got a call from the Utah Highway Patrol—"

"Utah? This isn't about Lena?"

An instant look of understanding crossed the big man's face. "No. It's not about Lena. It's not good, but it's not like that."

She took a deep breath of relief and then her brain began to race. Not Lena. Utah. "Jesse."

An image of Jesse's body broken and desic-cated by the climate filled her head and she quickly shoved it away. Her mother was right when she said Abby always thought the worst first. She closed her eyes for a moment. She'd have to find a way to change herself or one day she'd wake up unable to see the good in anything.

The sheriff nodded again. "Seems they found Jesse's car."

"His car? His car?" She stopped and took a deep breath. "I'm sorry, Sheriff. Where did they find his car?"

"Apparently Jesse loaned his car to one of the residents of Boulder. Boulder, Utah, that is, not Colorado. It's outside the area called Escalante Staircase National Monument." She nodded and the sheriff continued in his solemn, official tone. "The man said he dropped Jesse at a trailhead inside Escalante about two months ago and then came back every couple weeks and dropped off supplies at a designated spot, and for that he gets the use of Jesse's car."

She couldn't help but smile a bit. "That sounds very much like a Jesse-type bargain."

"The problem is when the man went to the drop-off point a few days ago, the supplies he left the last time were still there."

"And he didn't tell anyone about it right away?"

"Not until the State Patrol spotted Jesse's car and questioned him. From what the Utah officer said, the man's a bit like…" The sheriff paused and fingered his hat.

"Like Jesse."

He nodded.

Abby continued. "And no sign of Jesse has been found." It wasn't a question, it was more a pronouncement of the kind of life Jesse lived in spite of what it did to anyone else. *Oh, Jesse, you never mean any harm.*

"Not quite."

"Not quite?"

"Hikers found a backpack and some uneaten supplies." When she nodded, he reached into his shirt pocket and pulled out a photo.

She glanced at the photo. "That's his."

"You're sure?"

"Kyle gave him that little stuffed animal to take with him." She pointed to a small, now scruffy-looking, stuffed yellow ducky. Jesse had proudly hung it on the zipper pull of his backpack. "He said when the ducky got back, it would tell Kyle all about the trip, and then he…he spoke like Donald Duck. It's a thing the two of them did."

Her lips curled up at the thought of Jesse

and…his son. Was Kyle his son? Would he ever know? She had control of the tears now and refused to let them fill her eyes.

Sheriff Potts tucked the photo back in his pocket. "He's been listed as a missing person and they've notified all the proper authorities."

"Now what? Are they looking for him? Is there anything I can do?" She squeezed the fistful of tissue.

"All you can do right now is let us know if he turns up or you hear from him. I'm afraid there isn't the manpower available to do anything more than a cursory search. The national monuments have even less personnel than national parks. And Escalante is a big wilderness area." He paused and gave her a steady look of concern. "And now, I want you to understand this, Abby. Going there yourself isn't going to help anyone."

She nodded her understanding. "Why did you come to me and not his brother?"

"He left instructions for you to be contacted if he didn't return, and for you not to bother with his family unless you—and according to the man with Jesse's car, these are Jesse's words—'unless you want to get mixed up in that mess.'"

The sheriff made no further comment. And right now Abby loved him for it.

"Thank you, Sheriff. I'll let you know if I hear anything."

"If there is anything anyone can do for you, you let me know." She knew he meant it, about this, about anything, and where the sheriff "went" so would the rest of the town. Right now she felt closer to the people of St. Adelbert than she ever had.

The sheriff gave her a name and number of the man who had been leaving the supplies for Jesse, and she walked him out.

When she closed the door, she leaned against it and listened to the sound of his boot heels on the wooden porch. Helplessness was all she could feel. Jesse was officially missing and for some reason, she could no longer think of him as anyone but Kyle's father.

She pushed away from the door. Reed needed to be told about his brother being officially declared missing, and someday she'd have to tell Kyle...and Lena.

Reed first.

How to tell him, she didn't know, but when she checked outside, it became irrelevant. His car was gone.

FRED NIVENS WAS THE ONLY lead he hadn't followed up with, and now Reed stood outside the auto repair shop and waited while bearded Fred of Fix It Fred's wiped some of the grease from his hands. He wasn't surprised the auto shop was open on Sunday. People in St. Adelbert needed their cars during the week. No taxis. No buses.

The repair shop looked no worse for wear after the emergency mood of the phone call Fred had gotten at the diner the other day.

Reed had waited for forty-five minutes while Fred finished what he called a delicate operation. Reed took that to mean someone else was waiting for what Fred was doing. Reed had been there. It happened in the corporate world—well, most of the time. It just depended on how high up you were on the food chain. The first five minutes Reed had waited inside, but the smell of gasoline and other petroleum products had him thinking self-preservation dictated a change of venue.

Fred bustled outside. "So that little brother of yours has set this whole town to worrying."

"I'm afraid that's the truth."

"Too bad. Nice fella. Can't repair a car worth a damn, though. Wasn't even much good at changing the oil."

"I've been asking around to see if anybody has any hints about where he planned to go after hiking in Utah."

"Me? Got no clue, but I have a couple stories about the guy you might want to hear."

Fred sat down on the bench outside the shop and Reed sat beside him.

AFTER THE SUN HAD BEGUN to drop in the late-afternoon sky, Reed let himself back into the apartment above Abby's garage.

Fred had invited him to stick around and stay for dinner, but he had declined. Fred was a bachelor and if his home was anything like his cluttered shop, there must be a better choice. Reed wasn't feeling particularly sociable anymore. In fact, he had started to like being with himself. He felt more at peace with himself here in St. Adelbert. No wonder the residents loved being nestled in the mountains where the world had less of a chance to peck at them.

He suspected the Harveys had sent him to Fred to learn more about his brother and his brother's life than to find any information about where Jesse might be now. Strange and wise folk, those Harveys. Just wait, Abby had said. He had no idea Jesse had an interest in hunting and trapping or that he ever enjoyed reading anything, let alone American history. Fred gave him that and regaled him with many tales. One story was about the bear encounter in which Fred and Jesse had learned how fast they could climb a tree they would have normally thought to be unclimbable.

A tap on the door had him turning to see a mass of curling, dark hair backlit by what was left of the day's remaining sunlight. Abby.

He opened the door to let her in. "Hello, Abby."

She stood on the landing looking uncertain, sad and just a little bit cold in her pink short-sleeve shirt that skimmed the tops of her breasts provocatively. When the sun in this part of Montana fell, so did the temperature.

"Reed."

"Please, come in."

She stepped past him into the room. Her jeans clung perfectly to her butt and thighs and sandals showed off naked toenails, no paint. He definitely wasn't in Chicago.

"I have something to tell you." She didn't turn around.

Interesting, he thought. It sounded like the beginning of a confession. A feeling of disappointment surprised him. He still wanted Abby Fairbanks to be squeaky clean and above reproach on all levels. Probably not fair, but feelings were feelings.

He stepped around her to see her face and she looked at him.

"It's about Jesse," she said with apology in her tone.

His phone rang. "Excuse me." He looked at the screen. *Denny*. He muted the sound. He'd call him back later.

"This is my 'learn about Jesse' day," he told her. He had already gotten to like the adult Jesse had become, and he feared from Abby's tone, tales and stories might be all he'd have left to take home with him.

CHAPTER NINE

"WHAT IS IT, ABBY?"

"I'm so sorry, Reed."

"Let's sit." Reed indicated the chairs at his brother's small kitchen table instead of the shabby old couch with the big-flowered slipcover.

He snagged Jesse's T-shirt and shorts that earlier he had laid on the kitchen chair, and tossed them on the bed in the other room. When he returned, she was sitting with her hands in her lap and an expression of deep concern on her face.

"What's happening with Jesse?" he asked.

She looked up when he spoke and he thought he saw traces of tears in her eyes.

"They've declared him missing."

"Who declared him missing?" He pulled out the other chair and sat down. Across the table from him, she furrowed her dark brows and rested her hands on the table.

"The state of Utah. They notified the sheriff here this morning."

"So they found proof he was there." That was at least a better start than conjecture and hearsay as to where he went.

"And they found his things, but not him."

"Are they sure the things were Jesse's?" Of course they were, but he didn't know what else to think or say. He had no idea how to face never seeing his brother again, let alone tell their mother.

She nodded and studied her fingers. After a moment, she took a deep breath and told him of the untouched food, the loaned car and the apparently abandoned backpack with the stuffed duck attached to it.

The tentative way she laid out the grim news told him she counted herself among those who loved Jesse. A list that included practically everyone at the diner, Jesse's employers, the Harveys, probably Abby's sister, Lena—and one little boy. At least, by leaving Chicago, Jesse had found people who truly cared about him. He might be the smart one in the family.

As he thought about his brother, Reed understood he had not lost his brotherly love.

It had been tucked away with the rest of his childhood.

When Abby stopped speaking, she glanced up at him and he didn't like the distress he saw on her face.

"There's more?"

"The sheriff said the authorities in Utah, at Escalante, can't do much in the way of searching. They don't have the people and the area is too large. Too large for us to go there and help. I spoke with the man who has Jesse's car and he is going to make sure there are notices posted so anyone in the area will know to tell somebody if they see Jesse."

She bowed her head and swiped at the tears forming in her eyes. Tears for his brother? Abby Fairbanks didn't seem like the kind to cry at all.

She got up and started for the door.

He leaped to his feet and grabbed her hand, so she stopped and turned back toward him.

"What else is going on?" he asked.

"What?"

She seemed startled and then all the strength and determination he had known her to have fled, and she almost crumpled right in front of him. He pulled her to him and wrapped his arms around her.

Reed Maxwell the nurturer. He had no idea where that came from. Mountain air? No matter what else was going on, holding Abby felt like the right thing to do just then.

Standing here, with this woman in his arms, he realized she made him feel real, like a human being. His parents' home, always filled with the help, had never done it. His corner office overlooking Lake Michigan did not and neither did the corporate jet engender feelings of warmth and connection.

Mountain air. Mountain air explained everything. Didn't it?

She let him hold her for a moment longer and then pushed away. The tears dried up and she stood straight with her shoulders back and her chin held high.

There was the Abby Fairbanks he knew. He touched her cheek. "Tell me what else is going on."

Her shoulders relaxed. "It's really nothing or it's probably nothing, just me worrying."

"Your sister?"

She nodded.

He took her hand and tugged her across the

small room to the couch where he plopped down and pulled her down beside him. She managed to stay perched on the edge, so he scooted forward, put his arm around her back, and slouched until his head rested somewhat comically on her shoulder.

"What are you doing?" She tried to push his head away and he resisted.

"Our siblings have managed to make it so we need comforting. I thought we might as well comfort each other."

She stiffened under his cheek and then she put her hand on the side of his head and relaxed back on the couch, taking him with her.

They sat, or rather slouched, there until he thought she might have fallen asleep. When he lifted his head to look at her, she pulled his cheek back down to her shoulder.

"Tell me about Lena," he said. "First tell me about what's happening to worry you and then tell me all about her."

"She's missing, too, or rather she's overdue from a mission." She told him about the email, about the possibility Lena wasn't missing at all, but that the assignment was just more complicated than they thought it would be. "It's not like this kind of thing hasn't happened before. They usually don't know exactly how long they'll be gone. Things are always sort of fluid."

"And you haven't even told your mother."

"I can't. She thinks everything that goes wrong in her daughters' lives is because she somehow failed them. I'll tell her when I know something for sure."

He knew that one. He thought of what he told his own mother and what he kept to himself.

"Is Lena a good soldier?"

"She's a damned fine soldier, if trying hard counts. She says she has so much to make up for."

He lifted his head and pulled her closer to him until she was firmly tucked against his rib cage and thigh. "Now tell me about your sister, Lena."

She turned toward him, and when she put her hand on his chest, he covered it with his and wondered how long he could he sit there with her pressed into him, the smell of her, the strength of her. She invaded all his senses and his sensibilities. How long could he sit there without kissing her again? He had thought their first kisses had been a spur of the moment thing that couldn't really mean very much, but he felt another "moment" closing in fast and somehow the next kiss would mean more.

"My sister is the funniest, most aggravating person on the planet and there is no one who will love quicker or harder. She tells me I'm a saint."

He laughed. "Are you?"

"I might be—because it's not a compliment in Lena's book. She thinks I never do anything wrong and doesn't remember our mother ever punishing me."

"You were a lucky kid."

"I'm afraid the drugs might have affected Lena's brain." Then she laughed, a soft musical sound, and Reed couldn't help but want more of the sound, of her. The warmth of her body, the softness of her skin stirred things in him he didn't care to examine too closely.

"I'm kidding about the drugs," she continued. "I'm sure Lena tried them, but not enough to do that kind of damage."

"She didn't inhale?"

She laughed again. "She sucked them in as far as she could, but luckily, before she got addicted to anything, she learned they weren't making her life better."

"That's why she chose the army?" He didn't know why he asked a question to which he already knew the answer. Testing her? Distracting himself because he wanted to taste her?

"It was firmly suggested by a judge that she find some way to get her priorities in order."

"It seems to be working." Sudden, ridiculous relief flowed into him. She wasn't afraid of the truth, at least about her sister.

"That doesn't stop me from worrying insanely about her."

"So you're the insane saintly sister."

She laughed again. "And your brother and my sister are a couple of insensitive creeps."

"Yup. Total creeps." Just a nibble. He wanted just a nibble of her.

"We should do something to show them they can't drive us crazy no matter how hard they try."

"What should we do?" He brought her fingers to his lips and kissed each fingertip. Then he held his breath as she lifted her kissed fingertips to his cheek and kept them there while she leaned in to kiss him.

"This," she said against his lips. Her soft mouth opened against his and he slid his tongue in to meet hers. Just a nibble? He felt himself go hard. He usually had more control than that, but with Abby control seemed out of the question.

When she strained to get closer, he hauled her onto his lap with all the finesse of a caveman. The feeling of her pressing down as she settled on top of him almost sent him over the edge.

He pulled his mouth away and kissed a trail down her neck, down the V of her soft pink shirt to the enticing swell at the lowest dip of her shirt's neckline. When he brushed his palm against her breast, her nipple was as hard as he was.

They explored each other with tongues and hands and when she lifted his shirt and put her hands on his bare chest he knew he didn't just want her, he needed her, all of her.

"There's a bed here," he said without looking up.

"Are there condoms?"

He stopped what he was doing and lifted

his head. "I don't have any and I didn't see any in Jesse's things."

"Hmm. That would be a big 'no,' then, because I don't have any. I might be willing to risk a disease or two to satisfy my sudden need, but I won't risk a baby. Not fair to the child."

Was she thinking of Kyle when she said that?

"Oh, no." She giggled.

"Funny? You think this is funny." He grinned.

"Very. If either of us goes to the drug store for condoms we might as well put a big sign up in the town square that we're going to have sex."

He draped his arms over the back of the couch. "I wasn't in the mood for sex anyway."

She squirmed against him. "Yeah, right. Me, either."

He grabbed her and pulled her against him to try to stop the wiggling. "You have a very mean streak, Abby. So how trustworthy are we? We don't have to need condoms."

"I've always been told I'm good at adapting to difficult circumstances." She lifted her brows a bit and pursed her lips.

"So you're good when things get hard?"

"I am." She reached between his thighs and let her fingers be good with the hard thing she found between his legs.

He grabbed her around the waist and lifted her so she could no longer reach him. "There's a bed here in a room with a door."

"Good, because not everybody around here waits to be asked in after they knock, or even knocks for that matter."

He snapped his gaze toward the front door. Without a curtain, anyone on the landing could see what was happening in the living room.

So not at all like his condo in Chicago.

He lifted her to her feet and let her pull him up. As they stood toe to toe, he wrapped his arms around her and kissed her mouth, her neck, and nipped her nipple through her shirt and bra. All the time she pressed him toward the bedroom until they were inside and then she closed the door with the backward kick of her foot.

"I've never explored my landlady before," he said as he stepped toward her.

"I've only ever had one tenant before and the thought of exploring with him never occurred to me." She laughed as she kicked off her sandals and reached for the tail of her shirt. "Unless a virtual smack on the nose with a newspaper from time to time counts."

"It does not. Stop." He held up a hand and then sat down on the edge of the bed where he could get a better view. "Okay, continue."

She lifted her shirt until her face was momentarily hidden. A navel stud. There was so much of Abby Fairbanks to explore. She slowly tugged the shirt the rest of the way over her head, then she wiggled her jeans down and stepped out of them, a delectable pink bra dropped onto her clothes pile with a delicate plop. Freed, her full breasts swayed and her dark pink nipples turned upward beckoning him.

She stood in front of him dressed in only her panties and waited. He took the hint immediately and stripped to his boxers. It took about two point three seconds.

She smiled slowly. Then she placed her palms on her stomach and slid them lazily around to her hips and under the waistband of the panties.

"Wait."

"Again?" Her tone teased but she stopped.

"I want to unwrap that part myself."

He positioned her between his spread legs and she put her hands on his shoulders. When he lowered the back of her panties by sliding his hands down the soft, warm curve of her butt, she squeezed his shoulders and sighed.

This was wildly, insanely amazing and if it wasn't the mountain air it was the mountain woman driving him to a madness he didn't think he had in him.

After he had her panties off, he repositioned her so one of his thighs was between her legs. Then he reached around inside her thighs and slid his hands up to the treasure he had opened. He massaged her with his thumbs and her sighs turned to soft moans.

"Reed, I don't know if I can do this." She pushed her upper body back a little to look at him.

"You already are."

"I mean, I want you inside me so bad, I might just try to take what I want."

"Warning received, but let's see if we can do something about that." He leaned back and brought them down on the bed.

"Aunt Abby." Kyle's call came from far away, but not far enough.

"Where are you, Aunt Abby?"

She sat up. "They're here. Kyle and my mother."

"Maybe they'll go away."

"They'll search for me until they find me is what they'll do. In a few minutes he'll walk right in the apartment and into this room. Jesse used to let Kyle come and go anytime he wanted, so don't even expect a knock. Not that I didn't try to teach him to knock anyway."

"Jesse was never good with manners."

"I meant Kyle." She laughed and gave him a light fist to the chin. "But you knew that."

"We could put the dresser in front of the door."

"AAAbbeee." The sound came closer this time.

She laughed as she leaped up and started putting on her clothes. "Hurry. We have to get dressed."

He lay on the bed wearing only his boxers, his tented boxers.

"I'm afraid putting clothes on it isn't going to help much, at least not immediately. Unless you have a muumuu I could borrow."

She looked at him and said very seriously, "It would have to be a very large muumuu."

He got up and lifted her hair out of the neck of her shirt and then pulled her against him. "You go and I'll be along in a few minutes. Tell your mother I'm nearly naked. She'll understand."

"She'll cheer. Now let me go before Kyle gets a lesson he's way too young for."

He relaxed his arms, but instead of stepping away, she kissed him until he was ready to move furniture and to hell with the circumstances.

Too soon, she pushed away again to snap her jeans and slip on her sandals.

"MOTHER, I WAS JUST ABOUT to have dinner." Abby stood in the middle of her kitchen with her hands on her hips.

"Best news I've heard in years." Delanna's usually neat red hair flew about her shoulders. Having a five-year-old around you all day could do that.

"Bake a pizza and—"

"I can't find my pj's, Aunt Abby," Kyle called from upstairs.

"In your dresser," Abby called back and then addressed her mother. "And watch a movie."

"Get hot and make a movie. Better and better."

"Watch a movie, by myself."

"You do have to break my heart. You don't have to marry the guy. So why were you coming down from Reed's place?"

"He and I were having a conversation if you must know. Jesse was officially declared missing today." She recounted what the sheriff had told her. With every telling she realized not much had changed. She had already feared the worst for Jesse.

"You know I love Jesse as much as the next person," her mother said, "but the boy is a worry carrier. I decided that the first time I met him and then decided to love him when I could see him and the rest of the time, wish him well."

"You're a wise woman, Mother."

"So listen to your wise mother. What could be better in this valley than a piece of Reed Maxwell?"

"Okay. All right. Reed Maxwell is hot and if I were going to have sex with anyone tonight, it would be him."

Her mother slapped her on the back. "That's my girl."

"I said if."

"Well, I say go do it."

Her mother flicked something off Abby's shoulder and then pounded her hands flat on the table. "Kyle Fairbanks, I'm coming up there to get you in two seconds," she shouted.

Kyle laughed and then his footsteps pounded on the stairs. "I got Legos, too, Gramma."

ABBY SAT AT HER OWN KITCHEN table with her chin in her hands, elbows on the table.

The whirlwind Kyle had collected his pajamas and clean underwear, although he wasn't sure why he needed the clean underwear. He was only going to be gone for "a couple'a days, Aunt Aaaabby." Then grandmother and grandson left with as many Legos as they could carry.

Part of her wanted to go get Reed and take up where they'd left off. The sensible part wanted to give herself a "what were you thinking" swat on the back of the head. The kind her mother used to give Lena or her—see, her mother did punish her—when they had done something not really bad, but definitely out of line.

Was she out of line? Was she playing with something that could hurt them all? She could break her own heart and know she could mend it. She'd done it before, a couple times. Could she live with upsetting the status quo of Kyle's life?

Thank you, thank you, she said to herself, so glad there had been no condoms. Things could have become way too complicated for extraction without harm if they had. As it was they nearly...

Suddenly, it occurred to her she no longer thought of Reed as the interloper, the bad guy, the enemy. There must be some rational explanation for the private investigator in Denver, maybe Jesse. With a sinking feeling she knew it was time she told Reed her suspicions about Kyle and Jesse.

She got up and went to the back door.

As if she conjured him by thinking about him, Reed came down the wooden steps from the apartment. Now, why was her heart thudding madly as he strode across the lawn drawing closer to her with every step? Closer and closer and she got hotter and hotter. She held the door open, hoping she wouldn't scorch anyone or anything. Oh, Emma Harvey, did you start all this or just fan the flames?

"So how gone is the mood?" he asked as he entered

"Too much thinking under this bridge," she lied blatantly.

He leaned in and kissed her on the cheek, lingering a little longer than he needed to for a peck on the cheek. "Yeah, it's gone, and I'm hungry. Got any food?"

He didn't lie any better than she did.

"I have hot dogs and marshmallows." But she'd rather have him. Thank you. Thank you. She couldn't have him without paying a price she wasn't willing to pay.

"Hot dogs and marshmallows together?"

"No, silly. I had planned on bribing

Kyle with a cookout over an open fire if I didn't have the courage to let him go to my mother's."

"Is your mother a big scary ogre?"

"That would be me when it comes to Kyle. I can't seem to loosen my grip on him."

"Well, I'd like to be bribed with hot dogs and marshmallows." He ran a fingertip lightly along the edge of her jaw. "As long as there is ketchup. I can't eat hot dogs without ketchup."

His trailing finger moved down to her chest and before it could manage dangerous territory, she stepped away.

"I knew you liked ketchup. You were wearing it the first time we met."

He laughed. "No wonder I couldn't get you to take me seriously."

"Gourmet fare it is, then, with ketchup." She turned away and retrieved a long-stemmed butane lighter from an upper shelf.

"Take this." She handed him the lighter. "There is a fire already laid in the pit."

When he grabbed the lighter, he also grabbed her hand and it was all she could do to wiggle free and not accept the invitation.

"So you think I can light a fire, or are you trying to get rid of me?"

The fire he lit earlier had been fully stoked and was about to consume her. She quickly stepped farther away before he could touch her again.

"Go." She pointed at the door.

She put the food and the roasting forks, along with the fixings on a tray and was about to take them outside. Instead she stopped in the doorway and watched Reed. He stood in the light shed by the fire. The flames reflected off his dark hair and created dancing shadows across his face. He looked pensive. Fires could do that—cause thoughtfulness, and so could worry about his brother. And so could wondering if he had a nephew.

She pushed the door open with her elbow and strode across the grass to where she set the tray on the table positioned with two chairs near the small fire, and then faced Reed.

"There is still something I need to tell you."

He looked at her for a long moment. The reflection of flames danced in his eyes and the firelight cast a glow on his skin that had her clenching her fingers into fists so they would not reach out of their own accord and stroke where the flames cast magic.

"I don't need to hear it right now. How's that?"

"You do." Oh, courage don't fail me, don't fail me.

"Maybe, but right now I want to watch the stars and cook wieners over an open fire and burn marshmallows into little crunchy black puffs filled with goo."

"But it's important."

"That's why I don't want to hear it. Hot dogs and marshmallows and open fires are serious enough business."

She wanted to just blurt it out, but she also wanted to roast wieners and watch the stars with him. She looked up. "No stars, just clouds."

"Okay, then I just want to roast."

She was roasted, all the way through. Now that she had made the decision to tell him her suspicions, she just wanted to get it over with, cast away the pall the thoughts gave her. Cast the pall—on to him?

Let him have this night, uncomplicated

and easy. How many did anybody ever get in their life?

He sat down in one webbed lawn chair and pulled her down into the other. When he held a long fork out to her loaded with a hot dog, she took it, vowing not to let the decision fester inside her, but equally determined to let Reed have his evening of leisure. They weren't going anywhere. Kyle wasn't going anywhere and if Jesse was gone, things were likely to get a lot more complicated, and quickly.

They cooked and ate until they were both full. Then they relaxed in their chairs and watched the fire. The talk eventually came around to Jesse, about how they would each miss him if he were truly gone and it surprised them to find many of their reasons were the same. For instance, no matter what you did, Jesse always forgave you and never stopped loving you in his own way.

Reed reached out and stirred the flames. "That's the interesting thing about Jesse's carefree lifestyle. After a while, it sort of numbs those around him into a state of low-level worry."

They stared into the fire some more until

Reed said into the quiet of the night, "We're a lot alike, you and me."

She gave him a "you've got two heads" look. "Yeah, you and me. Alike."

"Okay, set the dollar amounts aside. We're both the responsible parties. Change the names. Change the location. You feel it's up to you to make sure the world around you is in order, and to see that everyone is safe. I'm here in Montana trying to set my family's world in order, make sure everyone is safe. You're doing the same."

"I guess that's true and does make us a bit alike."

"You do go a step further than I do, though. You want everyone to be happy. I settle for safe and secure."

She laughed, but what he said was fair. There really wasn't a time when she remembered that she did not somehow feel responsible for her family, her mother and sister, even Kyle. She dragged an unwilling Lena to prenatal visits and made sure she took her vitamins and ate properly.

"I even felt it was my fault for my father leaving. He got mad at mom for buying an expensive Christmas gift for me when I was

six and when she told him he was being selfish, he yelled at me and walked out the door.
I never saw him again."

"We differ there. I always knew my father
was never going to think of anyone except
himself and it took you at least six years to
find out."

"I'm afraid it took me a lot longer than that.
I might still feel a little responsible."

"Families are tough." He reached out and
ran a hand up her forearm to the pushed-up
sleeve of the jacket she had put on over the
light top. "So how else are we alike?"

"I think we—" The clouds chose that
moment to let loose large, cold raindrops.

"Yeow!" she cried when a big fat one
landed on her neck just above the jacket collar
and slid down her back.

"Run." She dumped the bucket of water
she had kept nearby onto the fire while Reed
grabbed the tray of dinner leavings. She made
a mad dash toward the house. Reed lagged
behind. She reached the porch overhang and
turned as the sky opened and doused Reed
when he was still a few yards out.

He ran, but too late.

Drenched and chuckling, he stepped up onto the porch.

"You coulda warned me."

"I thought 'run' meant the same thing in Chicago as it does here."

She held the door open for him to carry the tray inside. The bowl she had put the marshmallows in had a pool of whitish water in the bottom.

She thought to chide him for making marshmallow soup, but when she looked at him and the water dripping from his hair down onto his face, all she could do was laugh.

He looked steadily deadpan at her. "You do so laugh at things I do not think are funny."

"Don't make snap judgments about things you can't see," she said and laughed harder. Then she grabbed a towel from a nearby drawer, lofting it to him as he returned her laughter with a grin and began to dry his face and then his hair.

"Hot chocolate?"

He lifted one elbow to look at her as he continued to scrub his hair dry.

She pointed to the bowl of wet marshmallows. "Because that's all those puppies are going to be good for."

"Thanks." The single word sounded more like a growl.

She was sure, this time, his dark eyes actually sparkled with amusement.

"Thanks and yes to the hot chocolate or thanks for pointing out that a city guy doesn't know what 'run' means?"

"I'll pass on the chocolate."

"So it's the run thing, huh?"

"Does your mother control the rain?"

"My mother. What's my mother got to do with the rain?"

He pointed to her mother walking toward the house and apparently not a drop of rain was falling outside now. It was then she realized the pounding of the rain on the porch roof had stopped.

"I wonder what she wants." *And where's Kyle?* She started for the door.

He laid a hand on her shoulder. "Relax. She doesn't look troubled."

"Just determined."

Reed lowered his hand and stepped away to put the kitchen table between them. Abby felt the loss of his touch, but at the same time, glad her mother would not see them so close. She'd heard more than enough over the years. "Find a man, Abby. Stop using your life up on other people, Abby. Loosen up, Abby. Have a little sex once in a while." Her mother would exasperate and prod her—and prod.

Delanna Fairbanks strode into the kitchen.

"Mother? What are you doing here again and where's Kyle?"

"Chill, Abby. He's in the car." Her mother crossed the small kitchen without comment, and stopped abruptly to toss a brown paper bag on the table between Abby and Reed. "Nobody even blinks when I do it."

"Mother, what are you talking about?"

Delanna leaned toward her daughter and plucked at the seam on the shoulder of Abby's shirt. Then she walked out the back door.

"What the heck?" Abby put her hand on her shoulder. "Oh, my God!"

"What?" Reed was at her side in a flash.

"Oh, my God!"

"Abby?"

"I'm so sorry. I am so sorry." Her horror turned to laughter.

Reed smiled. "Abby?"

Abby grabbed the shoulder of her pink

shirt and showed him the stitched seam that should have been on the inside and then lifted the tail to show him the white polka dots that were. "Mother flicked me on the shoulder earlier before you came down. She was trying to tell me I had my shirt on inside out. Oh, my God!"

"Now what?"

Abby grabbed the bag, almost afraid to peek inside, but she did.

Tootsie Rolls?

"No doubt about it, my mother's crazy." To prove it, Abby dumped out the candy onto the tabletop.

The candy scattered and so did several brands of colorfully packaged condoms.

CHAPTER TEN

"MOTHER!" SHE CALLED, but Delanna was already in her car and pulling out onto the street.

Abby scooped frantically at the colorful pile, trying to shove the contents back in the bag. The more she grabbed the more they squirted between her fingers and flew in impossible directions.

She didn't ask herself how her mother could have done a thing like this. It was exactly the type of thing her mother would do.

Reed was polite enough to keep his chortling at a low pitch as he leaned down and picked up some of the escapees that had fallen to the floor. "Ecstasy and skin, spelled *s-k-y-n*. They're trendy at the drugstore in St. Adelbert."

Abby looked in horror to see him holding up the pair of condoms.

"Give me those." She made a grab, but he closed his fist.

"If only I'd had some of these with me earlier…but who would have thought I'd need them on a trip hunting for my brother."

"It's oddly reassuring to know you don't keep a supply at the ready," she said as she continued to recapture contraceptives.

"Oh, I always keep Tootsie Rolls in my shaving kit, just in case." He opened his hand and then he looked at the objects on his palm and then at her. With a grin, he pocketed the condoms and the Tootsie Rolls. "I almost didn't come down here because I thought we might have been getting into something we'd regret. But I came…no, wait, I didn't and that's why I'm here."

She gave him a sham shocked look.

He shrugged. "Hey, I'm a guy."

"I'm not a guy." She looked at him slyly as she dropped what she thought was the last of the condoms and candy into the bag and rolled the top down tightly. "And I might feel the same way."

He snapped up another stray condom and moved toward her.

"However…" She raised her hand.

He took hold of her hand, put the condom in it, and pressed the palm flat against his chest. "*However.* I don't think I like that word anymore."

"However," she said more firmly. "If we have sex right now, my mother will know."

"She brought condoms, so I think she gives us her blessing to be adults. Besides, if we don't have sex right now, what will she think?"

Abby hesitated for a moment. She wanted to protest, but the truth was the truth. "She'd think we're having sex right now."

He let a slow smile cross his face. "So if a couple is given condoms and they don't have sex, did they really not have sex?"

"If a tree falls in the forest..."

"Do you want to be...a tree?" He brushed his lips over hers.

"Mmm." A flood of yearning swiftly filled her and nearly overcame her sense of reason.

"Do you want me to leave?" He put his arms around her and she pressed close to him.

"You mean make like a tree?" She reveled

in the feeling of his arms around her. She didn't ever want him to leave.

"Trees are a little too sedentary for what comes into my mind when I have my arms around you, but I could just go back to the apartment."

"No, I don't want you to go back to the apartment." Then she closed her hand around the condom and looked directly into his eyes. "I don't think I've ever been very good at the woman-man thing."

"Because you've been busy?"

"Yeah, busy." Busy with making bad choices of men in her life. Busy trying to hold men at bay so she wouldn't turn out like her mother. Busy trying to be respected by the people around her. Busy with a misguided but lovable sister and with a boy who had her by the heartstrings long before he was born.

"How long have you felt responsible for the people around you?" Reed's voice broke into her thoughts.

"Forever." She cringed at how wistful her voice sounded.

"So you haven't taken much time for yourself."

She shook her head.

"How long has it been since you could just let go and be whimsical, be Abby?"

"Since, well, since Lena announced she was pregnant with Kyle. No, that's not true. I didn't do whimsical very well before that, either."

He stared at her for a moment, then he let go of her and stepped out onto the porch. From there he looked at the sky.

Then he took off for the apartment.

Great, Abby thought, *now I can make 'em just up and run away.* She tossed the condom up in the air and caught it. Then she put it in the bag with the others. *It's too bad, Mom, really too bad,* she thought.

She wiped away the ubiquitous water spots from the kitchen faucet and hung the towel on the oven door handle. Then she straightened the towel, twice, and then she was satisfied. Before she had time to clean more or to pick on herself any longer, Reed returned, took her hand and pulled her out the door.

He didn't say anything as he dragged her across the lawn toward the garage apartment, but instead of starting up the stairs, he veered away and headed toward his car.

When they were seated inside and he had

fastened the seat belt snuggly around her, she asked, "Where are we going?"

He didn't answer.

"You know even the diner in St. Adelbert is closed this time of night."

He turned to her. "One of the many things I've learned since I arrived in the Wild West is there is often a night show."

He backed the car away from the garage door and drove down the street heading toward the edge of town.

Night show. They weren't very far away from town when she realized he was taking her away from the light shed of the town to see the stars. It had been a long time since she had sat in the utter darkness and watched the night sky.

When they were a few miles out of town, he turned into a pullout in the road. As he did, a car passed spilling light all over the place.

She knew a better place.

"Reed, go just a little farther. There's a road into the mountains away from the headlights of the cars. There aren't a lot of people out here, but it's a sure thing that when you want dark, they will all get in their cars and drive by with their high beams on."

"As you wish."

She guided him to an old, rutted road.

"We should have brought my SUV," she said as they bounced slowly along.

"It's a rental."

They both laughed.

"Pull over there."

He stopped, shut the car off and leaped out. She scrambled to get her seat belt unfastened, but before she could get out of the car, he opened her door, reached in and picked her up. Another second later, she was perched on the warm hood of the car and he climbed up beside her.

"A most cooperative sky." He pointed up and sure enough the clouds had broken. Stars by the billions blinked in and out in the black velvet canopy. Dazzling.

"We're a little early, but if I'm remembering correctly…"

"What are you remembering?"

He wrapped his arm around her and pulled her back to lean on the windshield.

In near perfect darkness, they sat surrounded by the gentle scratching and rustling of nature's night and their own quiet breathing. Stars twinkled overhead and the waxing crescent moon hung low, partially obscured by the mountains to the west.

"I won't ever be tired of this," Abby said after a long silence. Reed's arm tightened around her. It was such a good feeling, one to be cherished, but not acted on right now.

Eventually, the moon dropped behind the jagged horizon, taking its light with it. More stars twinkled and the few remaining clouds continued to separate and seemed to move in opposite directions until they nearly cleared the sky. Had he known the moon would hide away leaving behind the starriest of skies?

Suddenly a bright streak of light flashed, there and gone so quickly Abby had to re-think it to really believe the meteor had been there. "The Perseids. Not bad at all for a man from the city."

He nudged her shoulder. "You Montana people take such luxuries for granted."

"We do." A large white streak split the sky with showers of sparkles falling from the main strip of light. "Oh, yes, thank you."

They watched with an occasional *oh* or *wow*.

"Do you suppose they're watching the sky?" Abby asked.

"Jesse and Lena? Yes, I think they are."

"Me, too. I don't dare let myself think anything else."

"Lena and Jesse are two of the luckiest people I know. They found you to worry about them."

"I don't know how lucky that makes them. I wish they were both here right now. They could do some explaining."

Tell him. Tell him.

He pulled her against him and kissed her temple with a long, lingering kiss. Then he pressed his lips to the little spot in front of her ear.

"You're not watching the meteors," she said instead.

"Hmm. No, I'm not, but city guys get easily distracted." He moved his mouth down to the bottom of her ear and then down her neck.

"Another meteor," Abby said and tried not to scrunch her shoulder as Reed nuzzled a ticklish spot on her neck.

"I saw it."

"You did not."

"I thought I did."

"It must be oxygen deprivation." She pushed at his shoulder and he turned away to lean against the windshield.

"Whatever it is, I like it." He pulled her close to his side where they sat waiting for hot and dangerous things to pass overhead.

Hot and dangerous. A feeling of giddy aliveness flooded Abby. Reed Maxwell was hot and dangerous. Dangerous to her sanity and her happiness and she wanted him.

Her body hummed with the excitement of being so close to him and she savored every nuance, mentally licked up every crumb. Almost afraid to move lest she break the mood, she sucked in shallow breaths while she riveted her eyes to the night sky.

Reed shifted slightly to kiss her on the mouth. That was better. Kissing him was so much better than thinking about anything else. He coaxed until she opened her lips and darted her tongue out to dance with his. He sat up farther and leaned over her. He put his hand on her knee. Slowly, he slid his palm up her thigh until he cupped her and massaged her until she moaned and covered his hand with hers to stop him.

He pulled his hand away and sat up beside

her. "Call me crazy, Abby, but I want you. I know I don't have much to offer a Montana woman, but I have me, here and now."

She looked up to see a meteor wink over his shoulder. "I can't." Not when she hadn't been totally honest with him, told him her suspicions about Kyle and Jesse. And when she did…

She wasn't sure in how many ways she could let her heart break and still find her way back to sanity.

He rolled off the hood and onto his feet. When she slid off the hood, he hugged her quickly and stepped away. Then he opened the car door and she slid in knowing she was most likely ending something that could have been the best thing in her life.

THE NEXT MORNING, LOUD pounding woke Reed. He stumbled out of the bedroom to see a FedEx driver on the landing. When Reed opened the door, the man held out an envelope. Reed almost wanted to refuse it. What was inside could cause turmoil in many lives.

As soon as he bid the driver goodbye, his phone burped the ring tone of a call from his mother. He tossed the envelope on the kitchen table and went to get the phone.

Their conversation was their usual. He told her nothing because he had nothing absolute to tell her and he walked while he talked. This time he had the envelope on the kitchen table to draw his attention from time to time.

"Is that it? Is that all you're going to tell me? Is that everything?" His mother's shrill voice reached out of his mobile phone and drilled straight into his brain.

If he gripped the handset any harder, it was going to implode. His mother meant well, as well as she was capable of anyway.

"Yes, Mother. I am telling you what I know."

"Reed Maxwell, I need to know everything."

"You do know everything," he said, and thought, *Everything I know for sure*. He shot a longing glance at the FedEx envelope sitting across the room on the kitchen table.

Since his mother hadn't mentioned Denny's visit to the house, his partner must have pulled off a miracle, sneaked in, got the photo from the housekeeper, and got away without Mother seeing him. Denny was good at everything he did, very good.

"Just because I'm thousands of miles away…" *Thousands of miles?* Reed needed to get his mother tactfully off the phone, if he…

"Reed? Reed?" His mother repeated his name impatiently. "I think I need to come out there."

"We did this already, Mother. The state of Montana is not ready for you."

"Oh, yes, I forgot."

The FedEx envelope called to him. Now if there *was* a miracle inside, his life might get easier…if Jesse and Kyle looked nothing alike. A picture of Abby bloomed inside his head, the feel of her lips on his…

"I need to go now, Mother."

"I don't know. You seem so far away and every time I hang up, I'm afraid I'll never hear from you again."

"I will be coming home, Mother. You know I will. I'll call you."

"I suppose I could let you go."

He picked up the FedEx envelope and put it down again. If he opened it and found what he thought he might find, news, he might have to lie to his mother and not just hedge. The last thing he wanted to give her was false hope.

When he had something concrete, he'd give it to her.

"That would be good, Mother. Goodbye."

"Goodbye, dear. Have a good day and call me soon. I think…"

"I love you, Mother." He shut down the call with only a wisp of remorse because he knew she wasn't really finished talking. She never was.

Instead of sitting down at the table, he continued to pace.

Instead of opening the envelope…

He thought about the softness of Abby's lips, the springtime smell of her creamy skin and curling dark hair, the feel of her body against his. She seemed so honest and so unencumbered by the rules of the games played between the women and men who jockeyed for position in his world.

He stopped and looked at the envelope. It could contain all the answers he needed. It could prove Abby Fairbanks was as she seemed, a devoted aunt and loving sister with no big secrets.

It could also provide evidence she was putting up a fantastic facade of innocence. She could be filled with as much deceit and avarice as those in his part of the stratosphere. But if Abby Fairbanks didn't have her feet on the ground, then who did?

If she was hiding Kyle's parentage, so much for not wanting anything from him. She would want him to leave this little piece of Montana and never look back. *If you leave me a contact number* she had said when he'd first arrived in St. Adelbert. In the parlance of his world, that often meant get out, don't call or write.

He thought of the clear, honest look in those light brown eyes. Was she a good deceiver?

Or was he full of it and ready to jump to conclusions all over the place because he needed to placate his mother?

He finally forced himself to sit in the chair. He'd fire anyone who worked for him who showed this much indecision, including himself. He wondered if the situation, the location, or the woman was helping to make him too crazy to think straight.

The information inside the envelope might give his mother a reason to come out of herself, give her a reason to enjoy what life she had left. It could also destroy Abby's already precarious world.

The contents might also adversely affect the sister in the war zone, a sister that Abby so carefully protected. He couldn't think about Abby or her sister now. The child would probably adapt. He and his brother had managed after all.

Disgusted with his own procrastination, he picked up the envelope, snapped off the opening strip.

Inside was a note and picture of Jesse and him as young children.

"I thought you might want the real thing and not a copy if you were going to make decisions based on the photo." It was signed, "Good luck, Denny."

He looked at the picture. Reed's hair had always been dark and less curly than Jesse's. Jesse's hair was blond and curled around his ears. They had been posed by a professional photographer with a pair of large toy bears, and the well-meaning photographer had colored their cheeks too rosy. They looked suitably goofy for their age and grinning because they were too young to know how hard the world could kick a couple of kids.

He stared at the picture. Did young Jesse look like Kyle Fairbanks as he had imagined?

He got up and went into the bedroom. The photo of Jesse, Lena, Kyle and Abby grinned back at him from the bedside table as if daring him to decide. He snatched it up.

Side by side, there was no doubt. The two boys looked enough alike to be father and son.

He slumped his shoulders and flopped down on the edge of the bed holding one of the pictures in each hand. Abby Fairbanks, how could she do this? He had to ask the question. Maybe that was what she was trying to tell him last night when he wouldn't let her.

He looked at his watch. It was just after noon. She'd still be at work.

He should leave today. Go to Utah no matter what the sheriff said. First he had to have a discussion with Abby.

ABBY SAT AT HER DESK in the clinic. The patients were gone, the charts were finished and she should go home, but all she could think about was Reed. All day, she had had the feeling he would be gone when she got home. Why would he stay? No one knew any more about Jesse. Would Reed go back home or to Utah?

As much as she wished she had depleted the supply from the little brown bag of condoms last night, she also wanted to hold on to her heart. If she let herself fall in love with Reed Maxwell...

Fall in love? She was nuts, so very nuts. What could possibly come of falling in love with Reed? He lived a half continent away. She'd like to think he could feel the same things for her as she felt for him, but though she could save a life in an emergency, efficiently bandage all wounds, and had even been known to throw a few stitches in from time to time, she had to admit she was not a very capable judge of how a man was feeling.

Two ex-fiancés followed by a resident doctor in Denver had pointed that out quite blatantly. When she had thought the resident was a trusted friend, he had pointed a finger at her for his mistake, a mistake that nearly cost a patient her life. Doctor versus nurse. They had stood behind the doctor. And because the patient was a prominent woman, her photo had been splashed all over the news. The lawsuit had been horrendous, but since Abby didn't have any money, all they took was her self-esteem and the hospital's check.

"Yo, Abby."

Abby looked up to see Dr. DeVane standing over her smiling.

"Finished, Doctor," she said and smiled at the very pregnant Dr. Maude DeVane who owned the clinic with her husband, Dr. Guy Daley.

"Me, too, Abby, and thanks for all your help today. You were your usual efficient self. Though maybe a little distracted from time to time?"

"I didn't mean for you to notice." Abby let out a long breath. "Lena's squad is overdue and there's been no word. And Jesse Maxwell has been officially declared missing."

"I'm sorry, Abby. Are you okay?"

"Yeah. So far I've been able to convince myself they're both okay, and Jesse's brother is here."

"I heard about the brother." Dr. DeVane smiled and shrugged one shoulder. "I was behind the pea display in the grocery story and one of your neighbors was there telling all."

"Ah, small-town living." Abby in no way wanted to know what her neighbors had to say about Reed. It wouldn't be relevant, as he'd be gone soon. "I wouldn't have it any other way."

"Me, either. I'll always be grateful to the town that could help me fall in love with the perfect man."

"Is the perfect man picking you up today?"

"We're driving to Kalispell for a checkup."

"Have you decided whether you are going to deliver here or there?"

"It's a tough one. Who'd have thought I'd be a pregnant woman first and a doctor second. Even with both of us, the jury is still out."

A tall, darkly handsome man walked into the clinic and Maude DeVane gave her husband such a smile it almost broke Abby's heart. Those two had started out as the most unlikely to even speak civilly to each other and ended up happy like this. Abby doubted Guy Daley even knew she was there. He had eyes only for his beautiful wife.

A few minutes later, as she headed out to her SUV. She thought she should be tired, but energy infused each step she took. Maybe that was what being around true love could do for a person. Energized or not, she was glad to leave the clinic for the day, glad there were no patients who needed hospitalization today. She would have been the on-call nurse who would have to wait for the transport unit to take the patient to the hospital in Kalispell.

When she got to her truck in the parking lot, Reed was sitting in his rental car waiting for her. Her steps faltered for a moment. More bad news? He got out of his car and came toward her.

"We have to talk."

"Okay. I don't know why, but all day today I thought I might come home and find you gone."

He stopped in front of her and looked at her for a long moment as if trying to decide something about her.

"Can we find some place neutral to talk?" he asked.

That seemed ominous. "All right. There's a path by the river—is that good enough?"

He nodded and took her arm, and she led them out front of the clinic and across the street. Vala was standing in the window of the diner. She waved to them. Abby waved back. Why did she feel as if she were being led to her own execution?

Flickers of images of photographers pressing in on her flitted through her mind. The dark wave of anxiety these images usually caused tried to intrude, but she pushed back this time, hard, and the wave subsided. At least she had control of something in her life.

As they passed the drugstore, Mrs. Taylor smiled and Abby smiled. Just before the turn-off to the path, John Miller from the hardware store and his friend passed on the other side of the street. They also waved and Abby responded. Reed walked silently beside her holding her arm.

When they reached the path by the river, the water burbled quietly as it passed over the rocks. A few leaves floated like pea-green boats downstream and squirrels played in the branches of the trees above their heads.

When she could take the silence no more, she stopped and made Reed face her.

"I almost did leave today," he said in a restrained tone.

"And you didn't because?"

Instead of answering, he pulled something from his pocket. Abby looked at it for a moment and realized only that it was an old photo, in sepia tones with color added by hand. The photo was of two young boys. And then she looked closer. Kyle. No.

She looked up at Reed.

"Wow" was the most profound thing she could think to say.

"Did you know?"

She started walking down the path.

"Abby, did you know?" he called after her.

"Did I know what?" Could looks like that be coincidental? There seemed to be nothing she knew for sure.

"Did you know about Kyle and Jesse?"

"Is that—" she pointed at the picture he still held "—why you had a private investigator checking into me in Denver?"

"I don't know what you're talking about."

"Why don't I believe that?"

"How could you not tell me? No, wait. I get why you didn't tell me. But is that fair to the boy?"

"I suppose, if he is Jesse's son he should be taken to the Midwest where he could be rich enough to be raised by nannies."

"I don't think that's your decision to make."

"No, it's my sister's decision."

"Or my brother's."

"The picture doesn't change anything."

"You knew."

"All I ever had were unfounded suspicions. That's all I have now." She couldn't disrupt the boy's life because of a picture.

"Abby, you have to face facts."

"Face facts? Jesse is missing. Lena is missing. Those are the facts I have. And what if they're gone, Reed?" Her voice was suddenly so small it barely carried above the sound of the water.

"There's a woman back in Evanston, Illinois, who deserves to know she has a grandchild. She deserves to know she has another chance to get things right."

"Even if that's true, does that child, that five-year-old deserve to be somebody's chance—I am so sorry, but I have to be there for him. Does he deserve to be somebody's chance to mess things up again?"

"There's not a perfect answer here."

"I'm sure your intentions toward Kyle are honorable, but if you decide to fight me and my mother, and even Lena, I'm sure you have the power and the money to get whatever you want."

"I did not come here to break up anybody's family."

"Then don't do it."

"She's on a downward spiral and if Jesse is truly gone, there may be only one way to stop it or even to slow it down."

Abby felt the tears on her cheeks before she even knew she was crying.

"If he's Jesse's son, does Kyle get any say?"

"He's a child. He can't possible know what's best."

She smiled when she thought of Kyle, how bright he was, how wise he seemed at times. She thought of him in the bunny slippers and of how he thought his mommy might be afraid.

"I'd be scared if I had to go and live with

strangers—that's what he said the other day. He was thinking about his mother in the army and about how she was with so many people she didn't know. I'd be scared."

"You don't play fair."

"I guess we both use what we have, and what I have is the happiness and welfare of one little boy with a great big heart to think of."

She turned and hurried back up the path and down the street to her car. She drove home with purpose and when she stopped in front of her own garage, she wiped away the tears. If she had to fight, so be it.

"Abby. Abby." Her mother called out the kitchen door and waved to her as Abby got out of her car. "Good news."

Good news—she could use some good news to help loosen the knot in her chest that was once her heart. "Hang on, Mom. I'll be there in a minute."

"Aunt Abby." Kyle ran from the house and into her arms.

"What did you and Gramma do today?" she asked, hoping she could distract herself and forget about the picture.

"We played with Legos and we went to see the tow truck and guess what?"

"What?" It was hard not to catch his enthusiasm.

"The tow truck guy said I could go for a ride someday and we had those waffles for lunch."

"The tow truck man's name is Mr. Nivens and waffles sound so good." Abby collected her purse and headed for the house.

"And then we went to the park and then we walked here, but the other kids were going back to the park after dinner. Can I go back to the park? Can I?"

Kyle's eyes suddenly lit up. "Reed," he shouted.

Abby turned to see Reed's rental car approaching. As he pulled into the driveway, Abby grabbed Kyle's hand to keep him from darting toward the moving car.

Reed smiled as he got out, but Abby couldn't find a smile anywhere. Her reserve had been drained by the sight of the man who could make her soar one minute and then make her crash and burn. The man who could make her betray her sister's trust and take away the reason her mother felt as if she could face the world as a responsible adult.

"Hi, Reed!" Kyle tugged his hand away from hers and ran around the car toward the man who was his uncle.

CHAPTER ELEVEN

"HI, REED," HER MOTHER shouted from the back doorway, and then waved wildly at Abby with a plastic spatula in her hand. "Abby, come here."

Abby gave her mother a backhanded wave as she leaned into her SUV to pick up the ever-present trash from the floor. Reed listened politely to Kyle and seemed truly interested. Was he interested in Kyle's words or interested in befriending the boy so it would be easier to take him away?

Reed had listened so attentively to her last night. Been so empathetic. She should have told him her suspicions, no matter what the cost.

Please let him be a good person, please.

She watched Reed as he squatted down to listen to Kyle, to speak eye to eye with him.

He must think they all know Kyle and Jesse are family. What must he think of them?

"Abby. Abby are you deaf?"

She closed the hatchback and stepped away.

"I can hear you just fine, Mother. I'll be there in a second." She turned to Kyle. "Kyle, honey, it's time to come in the house."

"But Reed said he'd take me to the park for a while. Can I go, please?"

She looked at Reed and tried hard not to glare. He looked innocent, not like a sneaking, conniving uncle.

"Not now. It's getting kind of late."

"It's only quarter after six, Abbs. He ate a good dinner." Her mother accentuated her words with the dish towel she held in her hand.

"Can I go?" Kyle charged in between Abby and her mother. "Puh-leeese? Angus will be there."

"Kyle, go wash the dirt off your face. Grandma and I need to talk for a minute."

"Okay." The boy ran into the house.

"I don't mind, really. He's a cute kid." Reed entered the conversation and Abby didn't turn to acknowledge him.

She curled her fingers into her palms, made fists and squeezed. She could handle this.

One way or another, she had handled every-thing that had come her way. "That's nice of you, Reed, but I'll take him," she said, turn-ing to present him with the friendly smile she had forced onto her face.

"No," Kyle cried as he flew off the porch. "It's a guy thing. We want to do a guy thing."

Did the sky darken a little? Abby looked up at the blazing blue above. No, but her world had. Kyle deserved a man in his life. Every child deserved a man and a woman to learn from, to love them. But Reed Maxwell?

"Aunt Abby—" Kyle started again.

"Aunt Abby," Reed interrupted, "is being cautious and she should be, that's what adults do."

Abby speculated whether that was some sort of apology.

Her mother poked her on the arm. "It is nice of him to offer, Abby, and you need to stay here. I have to talk to you."

Abby looked at her mother, then at Reed and then at Kyle and turned back to her mother.

Kyle jumped up and down and her mother took her silence as acquiescence. Delanna glanced over Abby's shoulder at Reed and pointed off to the south as she continued, "The park is two blocks that way. It's really the playground at the school. And please be careful. Five-year-olds aren't for the faint of heart."

"Yippee! Com'on, Reed. Com'on. Angus'll be waiting for me."

Kyle dragged a grinning Reed away as Abby watched, feeling an ominous sense of loss that she hoped would never become permanent.

"Abby, what's the matter with you? Why do you look so strange?"

"I am strange, Mother. You've told me so many times."

"Not strange, weird. Are you sure you're okay?"

"I am, Mother." *I am. I am okay,* she repeated to herself. *I am and so is Kyle and so are Lena and Jesse.* "What are you doing here anyway? I thought you were going to keep Kyle again tonight."

"I was. I am, but this opportunity came up and—well, it's a time's-a-wasting thing for me. Besides, I wasn't kidding about that faint-hearted stuff."

"Do you know who that man could be?"

Her mother gave her a cautious look as if she knew she was answering a trick question and, without having any details, afraid of what the real answer would be. "He's Jesse's brother. Have you gone completely nuts?"

"Kyle could be Jesse's son."

Her mother froze for a moment and then a big smile spread across her face. "What do you know about that? I was always suspicious why Lena dragged Jesse to the back side of beyond with her. How long have you known?"

"I've always suspected. Although Lena never said, but Reed has this photo." Abby paused to take a breath. "There are two boys in the photo and one of them is Jesse, who, as a kid, looks so much like Kyle it's scary."

"Did Jesse have this all along?"

"No. I would have seen it if he did. Reed must have brought it with him, and if he did, then he came looking for a child. And if he has been looking for a child all along, I don't know what that means." What it could mean brought dread. It could mean he'd been using her all along.

"You're paranoid, Abby. Why would Jesse's

brother even suspect Jesse had a child? Jesse didn't know."

"I'm not sure." Abby shrugged. "Maybe Jesse had suspicions like I did and passed them on to his family."

"Maybe Reed brought the picture because he thought he could get Jesse to go down memory lane, make him want to be a part of the family again, and I thought Jesse hadn't talked to his family in a long time."

"He might have suspected when Lena was pregnant or when Kyle was younger and he told someone in his family then." The memory lane stuff might be plausible. Abby didn't know what to think.

"Well, if Jesse is Kyle's father, it's great." Her mother grinned and tossed a clump of auburn hair off her forehead.

"Will you think it's great when Kyle's uncle sues for custody and takes Kyle away to live in Chicago?"

"Why do you always have to believe in the worst?"

"Because when I believe in anything else, I get smacked in the face, that's why."

"That seems to happen a lot to you," her mother agreed and wrapped her arms around her daughter. "Life has been hard on you, yet you've always taken on everybody's troubles—mine, Lena's, even Jesse's. I was never surprised when you decided to become a nurse."

Abby hugged her mother back. "Thanks for noticing, Mom."

"Now." Her mother stepped away and then sat on the porch where she pointed to the spot beside her. "Sit. Talk to me."

"What are you up to, Mother?"

"You'll need to get gussied up tomorrow evening. The undertakers are—"

"Funeral directors."

"Are taking us out tomorrow night. They are taking us out to dinner."

"Mother, one night you give me condoms and the next day you get me fixed up with another man."

"I knew you wouldn't use them."

Abby almost wished she had used them at the time when she was still able to convince herself Reed was a hot guy and Jesse's nice older brother, not a rat. "Then why—"

"A mother can always hope. Now, young Travis is just right for you. He's quiet, dresses conservatively, has a good job, drives a nice new car and he lives right here in St. Adelbert. He's a nice, responsible young man. What more could you want?"

A little sex appeal, some personality, less girth, like Reed, only the good, upstanding parts of Travis should be kept. "You can't expect me to just drop everything to go out with a guy who asks at the last minute."

"Yeah, and you with all your important things to do tomorrow. You gotta polish your hiking boots or something? Besides, I think Travis is so cute in his volunteer firefighter uniform."

"Do they call those outfits uniforms? And he didn't even ask me."

"Who cares what they call them, and Kenny and I decided it would be best to just tell you and Travis you were going with us to the opening of the new restaurant in Franksville."

"All the way over in Franksville? I can't leave. What if Reed tries to take Kyle away while we're out on a date? What would I tell Lena? How terrified would Kyle be to find himself whisked away to some strange place? When would we see him again?" Bleakness washed through Abby.

"Don't be ridiculous. Reed's been here for nearly a week and he hasn't done a snatch and run. What makes today different?"

"He's been—"

Her mother sucked in a long juicy breath between her teeth. "You *did* use the condoms! Who'd a thought? Are you falling for him? Is that it? You fall for a guy so you think he must be some creepy loser. The kind you always pick. That'd be my fault. God only knows I paraded enough dead beats in front of you and Lena."

Abby knew she had fallen for Reed, but that was in the past. As long as Kyle was a child and as long as his mother was away, she would care for the boy, put him first.

"You've reformed, Mother. Kenny Fuller is a good man. Why don't the two of you go out?"

"Kenny is only going so his son will go out with you. You're a catch, you know, and don't think I didn't notice you dodged my questions about falling for Reed."

"Why do we have to do this now?"

"Tomorrow is the 'not to be missed' grand opening of the new restaurant in Franksville, and when something new actually happens around here it should not be—well—missed. It's what I used to convince Kenny we should all go."

"I don't know."

"What makes you think Reed will take Kyle away even if he is the boy's uncle?"

"I don't know anything for sure, but…"

"Well, nobody can fix everything. Now, what all are you going to wear for our date?"

"Am I talked into going?"

"I know I've not been the best of mothers, but I'm trying very hard. For me, Abby. Do it for me." Her mother fluttered her eyelashes and stuck out her bottom lip.

"You're not fooling anyone," Abby said as she gently tugged a lock of her mother's thick hair. Her mother would kid and beg in a silly way and otherwise skirt the truth that she desperately wanted someone to grow old with, a pal, a buddy and a lover. Kenny Fuller could be just that and he'd been a widow for a year now—fair game.

"I have nothing to wear, Mother."

"I'm sure wearing nothing would please Travis Fuller just fine, daughter. So you'll go?"

Abby pushed herself up from the porch.

"I'll go. What are you wearing, Mom?"

"I bought a new dress."

"So sure of me, were you?"

"I'm your mom."

"That you are." She wanted to trust Reed as she had trusted him last night when they watched the meteors streak across the sky, when he had held her and understood there were too many unresolved issues for them to use the condoms.... "What if Reed takes Kyle?"

"We can fix that."

"Are we going to tie him up?"

"Sort of."

"Mother?"

"Abby. We'll get him to babysit Kyle."

"And that will help how?"

"We'll promise Kyle that Reed will take him to the park again." Delanna stopped Abby's protest with a look. "When he's gone we'll park your car and his car in the garage, just in case it rains, of course."

"Of course."

"Resources around here are sparse, so it'd be several hours before he could have someone come and get him and I promise, we'll have a quick dinner and get back before you know it. All we need to do is put your spare door opener and all the keys where Reed and Kyle can't find them."

"What if he breaks the door down and hot-wires the car?"

"Have you seen any hint that Reed Max-well is a barbarian and a thug?"

"Hmm."

Her mother, in turn, swatted her on the arm.

REED SAT ON THE PARK BENCH beside a woman and a tiny baby. The park teemed with kids trying to stuff a little more summer into their lives, running, climbing, shouting and occasionally coming over to a parent with an injury, real or imagined. Reed enjoyed the camaraderie of the adults as they kept vigil. They greeted him as if he belonged. He'd obviously been in town long enough for the parents to know who he was and he basked in the halo effect of his brother's kind-spirited personality.

He thought he'd come to do guy things, but apparently, Kyle's ploy was to leave Aunt Abby behind. So he'd been told to "sit there, Reed" and had obeyed. Who'd have thought

Reed Maxwell of Maxwell and Anderson Investments, LLC would follow the commands of a five-year-old and then feel comfortable sitting on a park bench beside a woman feeding her infant.

Abby must do this all the time, bring the boy to the park. As he watched the children play, he realized how little credit he had ever given to people who took on the job of raising children. He wondered if he'd ever want to take care of a child.

He supposed he might, if the child were his and especially if he loved the child's mother.

Abby holding a baby flashed into his mind. Yes, Abby Fairbanks would make a good mother. She made an excellent stand-in mother for Kyle.

Reed watched Kyle streak across the grass chasing the soccer ball with his friends. His blond curls bounced and flew around his face the way Jesse's had. From his shirt pocket, Reed slid the supplies Denny had told him he'd need to collect a DNA sample from the boy. He already had one of Jesse's.

He thought of the look on Abby's face when she found out what he had done—and she would find out. He could collect the sample, but he couldn't bring himself to try to coerce the boy into complicity. The best he could do was not to make a big deal out of collecting the sample and hope the boy didn't mention it for a day or two, until Reed could plan what to do next.

If Abby found out, would she run?

"Reed. Reed, watch this," Kyle called from out on the field of soccer play. He kicked and the ball flew past a short-armed goalie about Kyle's size.

"You'll block it next time, Angus," the mother on the bench called to the goalie, who was now dejected and on the ground.

"They are so cute," the mother said, addressing Reed.

"Earnest."

"Yes, they are."

And honest, Reed thought. And so was Abby—at least honest in her passion to protect Kyle, and that was why she wouldn't run. She might think about it, but she'd weigh the reality of life on the run against life without the boy in it part-time. She would fight him with every weapon she had and she was right—those were few.

Maybe she'd consider moving to the Midwest to be closer to the boy. He looked out over the mountains, inhaled the clean air. She'd be crazy to do that. Maybe she'd find a man here and have children of her own, lots of them and make her loss of control over Kyle's life seem less dire.

She was absolutely right about one thing. Nannies were out. If he had to run his business from home, Kyle would have a relative with him, not someone paid to care for him, a someone who might change as often as the leaves on the trees.

Two days, Denny had said, from the time the samples hit the DNA laboratory—in two days he could have standard parentage DNA test results. He could stay in St. Adelbert for that long if he thought he had to for the boy's sake.

THE FOLLOWING EVENING, Abby tried to feel comfortable on the ride to the next town for the not-to-be-missed restaurant grand opening. It hadn't been hard to talk Reed into taking care of Kyle, and they had taken off down the street, holding hands and eating Tootsie Pops. Abby felt silly while her mother parked the vehicles in the garage and locked the door, but she couldn't force herself to resist, either.

The double date had started off as well as could be expected. The Fuller men wore sport coats with string ties and jeans on their date. They looked quite Western, handsome even, for a pair of undertakers. Abby would have bet that they each had a Stetson at home somewhere or even in the trunk of the car. Delanna wore a simple but elegant black dress, and her favorite strappy black stilettos. Abby chose a white brushed denim skirt that fell a few inches above her knees and a bright green blouse to compliment her hair color, her mother's idea, and a pair of comfortable sandals, her own idea.

They talked about things of general interest, but it wasn't enough to distract her from what her mind insisted on returning to. Reed. He hadn't left town as she suspected and he was especially nice to her and caring about Kyle. It was almost as if the difficulties were behind them and they could be friends now.

But was it real?

With every mile that took her away from Reed, she had to try harder to divert her mind, but whenever she thought she had been successful in temporarily forgetting the man, a flash of the two of them in crisp, unsettling detail brought it all back to her.

She smoothed the imaginary wrinkles from her skirt for what seemed like the hundredth time, and this time her date noticed and smiled kindly at her. Kindness. Travis was a kind man. Maybe she could learn to love him. For now, she'd have to find some other way to fidget.

In answer, her mind pulled up an image of Reed's dark eyes sparkling with amusement as he stood in her kitchen soaked with rain, his deliberate, sexy grin when he was plotting to take her out to stare at the stars. The touch of his hand alone was memorable, never mind the sensation of his soft and then demanding lips.

What would life be like shared with the man Reed had been two nights ago. She had never felt so cherished, so important. He had treated her the way she imagined a man should treat a woman, but had always believed was some kind of fairy tale.

Maybe they could be friends, and lovers, and maybe they could even end up together.

She saw herself flying across country to visit Chicago. Maybe they'd live in Montana. Reed could commute, conduct business from his plane so he wouldn't lose a lot of time while traveling.

Sure, sure, they could have a dream life. And as soon as she got back to the clinic, she could have her head examined.

The car's occupants laughed as if she had said the last thought out loud. Abby looked up and then looked back at her mother.

"We're laughing at you, Abbs. Kenny asked you if you were going to compete in the county-wide bake off next week."

"Sorry, I wasn't listening."

"We know, because then I asked and then Travis asked."

Abby felt her cheeks get hot. "Okay, you caught me. I was…" Thinking about the most intriguing man she ever met and wondering how she'd ever be able to settle for anyone else. *I'm so very sorry, Travis,* she thought. "Thinking about one of the patients at the clinic today."

"So are you?" her mother prodded.

"I would, but I don't have the time. Why don't you enter, Mother?"

Before her mother could retort, a sheriff's squad rounded the curve ahead with lights flashing. It whipped passed them at high speed and disappeared around the curve behind them.

"Wow!" Travis said. "He was in a hurry."

"Yeah, I hope it's nothing serious." Kenny said aloud the thought they were all thinking. A racing squad car could mean a friend or neighbor was in jeopardy.

Abby wasn't on call but everyone from the clinic would always volunteer to come in whenever something big happened.

A second squad car approached and passed at the same high rate of speed.

"That was the sheriff from the next county."

Minutes later, Travis's satellite phone rang. He pulled over and answered in clipped responses.

"I'm ten minutes out," he said, and ended the call.

Abby held her breath.

"We're going to move fast," Travis announced to them, then brought the big Ford around and sped up toward town.

"What is it, Travis?" Abby asked.

"There was an explosion and now a fire at Fred's shop."

"Oh, no," her mother whispered from the backseat.

"Mother?"

"Kyle was begging Reed to take him to see the tow truck."

Abby looked at Travis, who handed her his phone without her having to ask. Abby dialed home—there was no answer.

"Well?" her mother asked from the backseat, even though it was obvious.

She shook her head. "That doesn't have to mean anything, but I don't know his cell number."

From the backseat Kenny handed her Reed's business card. "He gave them out at the diner the other day."

Abby fumbled with the card for a moment, but quickly dialed.

Voice mail on the first ring. Either his phone was off or...

CHAPTER TWELVE

AS THE BIG BLACK CAR RACED back to town, Abby used the focusing skills she had learned as a trauma nurse in Denver to keep her mind from painting all sorts of disaster scenarios involving Kyle and Reed. Be prepared for anything, but deal with what's real and in front of you.

She would never find the words to tell Lena if something happened to Kyle at home in Montana where it's supposed to be safe. Both mother and son had to be safe. *Please, come back to us, Lena.*

While her mother and Kenny spoke quietly in the backseat and Travis drove with intent, she tried to picture the scene. How many people would have been at Fred's? Maybe they had all gone home to dinner.

Please let Kyle be okay. Please let them all be okay. There was not a person in town whose welfare she did not care about. Even

Reed. He might have her exasperated and frustrated in more ways than one and even frightened her a little when it came to Kyle, but she did not wish him any harm.

As they approached the edge of town, they could see flames licking up at the base of the column of dark smoke.

"Do you want to go directly to the clinic?"

Abby realized Travis's question was addressed to her. The two buildings weren't far apart, but minutes could make a huge difference in an emergency. Her heart told her to go to the explosion, but her logical mind told her the most seriously injured would already be or soon be at the clinic where the medical staff had the equipment to save their lives. If she were needed it would most likely be there. "The clinic, please, Travis, and thank you."

Travis nodded. "If I hear anything about Kyle, I'll get word to you."

You're a good man, Travis Fuller.

"I'll see to Kyle when we find him," her mother said.

"Thanks," she said to both of them.

Travis soon stopped the big Ford in front of the Avery Clinic.

"I'll call you when I can, Mom," Abby said as she hopped out of the car that sped away as soon as she slammed the door.

The clinic's glass-and-aluminum doors slid open automatically and the angry crying of a baby greeted her.

People milled near the waiting room door, and Fred Nivens paced the length of the entryway. He looked unharmed, thank goodness.

She stopped abruptly to see if she could spot the area of greatest need.

The department was set up with a central control area and treatment rooms arranged around the perimeter. Most of the time, the clinic served non-emergency office visits, but when needed a doctor, a nurse and a tech were always on call.

Off to the left, in the major trauma room, Dr. Guy Daley and a nurse leaned over someone, a woman, and in the pediatric room, Dr. Maude DeVane, assisted by a tech, checked the angry, squalling baby. The baby's mother, Angus's mother, stood beside the exam table with tears streaming through the grime on her face. Another tech was in the adjacent room posing the portable X-ray equipment over a blond child's lower leg. Kyle's friend Angus. His father stood a watchful guard over the boy.

An EMT stood beside a man still on a transport cart, a gray-haired man holding a bandage to his head. Mr. Taylor from the drugstore. Mrs. Taylor at his side.

No Kyle. No Reed.

Best-case scenario or worst? The dead would be brought last or not at all—but she wasn't going there. The uninjured would be sent home. Kyle would be at home and her mother would have hurried there by now. Reed would be with them. They would all be fine.

She'd hold that thought. Her heart couldn't stand anything else.

She donned a disposable surgical gown and secured it to protect her clothes. Before she found a place to insert herself into the fray, the doors behind her burst open. Baylor Doyle in his firefighter's gear and with a bandaged hand was leading Reed by the arm.

"Baylor. Reed."

Abby grabbed a wheelchair and rushed toward the pair.

Baylor helped Reed sit.

"See to him, I'll be all right," Baylor said and then patted Reed on the shoulder. "Thanks for your help, buddy, and you might want to keep leaning forward a bit."

Reed rested his elbows on his knees. When he did, Abby could see the tear and the darker stain of blood on the back of his shirt. The wound was in the middle of his back and to the right of midline.

"How are you feeling, Reed?" Abby asked and she tried to examine the wound. If he was short of breath or had any loss of feeling or movement below the wound, he could be in real trouble.

"I didn't think it was much, but I can't see back there, you know." He gave her a strained smile.

"He's a quick study and a good second man on a hose, but he needs somebody to watch his back," Baylor said and smiled.

Baylor always made things feel safer.

"How did this happen?" she asked as she pushed the wheelchair toward a treatment room. How it happened would also dictate how serious the wound might be. Every scrap of information could help save a trauma patient's life. If the wound was deep, Reed might have to be stabilized and airlifted to the hospital in Kalispell.

"He must have gotten hit during the explosion or when the debris fell."

"You were there during the explosion?"

"Kyle's fine. He's with your neighbors Cora and Ethel."

"Now answer my question. How do you feel?"

"It stung a bit when it happened," Reed said as he turned his head and smiled to reassure her, "but it's starting to hurt more now."

"Hi, Abby," Dr. DeVane said from the doorway of the treatment room. "What do we have here?" She came forward and warmly greeted Reed.

Abby quickly stepped aside and let the doctor look at Reed's back. When she was finished, she spoke to Abby. "Abby, I'll send a tech in to take some X-rays. Meanwhile, please check his vitals and we'll go from there." Dr. DeVane then turned to Baylor. "Let me see what you've got under that bandage, okay?"

Baylor followed Dr. DeVane from the room and Abby turned to Reed.

"I'm going to take your blood pressure and pulse while you're sitting in the chair."

As she jotted down the vital signs, she observed him from where he couldn't see her. If something dire happened to Reed, the world, her world, would be less bright, hold less promise. No other man in her life had ever made her feel that way.

"So far, Reed, everything looks great. Do you think you can get up and sit on the exam table?"

He agreed and she held his arm as he stood.

"We went to see the tow truck," he told her as he eased himself down to sit on the edge of the table. "Except for being scared out of his wits, Kyle's fine."

"My mother will be with him by now."

She helped him to recline onto his stomach. "Better?"

"Yeah. Thanks, Abby."

"Tell me about what happened."

"It's true. That kind of thing happens so fast. Fred had Kyle and Angus and I were in the tow truck. They were pretending to tow a car. He's a big old tame bear, Fred is."

"I'm going to cut your shirt off. You aren't going to want it anyway. Are you?"

"No. I was sitting on the bench in front of the shop. The building blunted most of the force of the explosion. Angus's mother and baby sister were there with me. There were some men in the shop with the mechanic. The HVAC men were in the back doing something—I thought—with the furnace. Suddenly it felt like Armageddon and then there was almost a moment of quiet, but I'm sure I'm exaggerating. Then the smoke started pouring out of the building and people were running away. A second or two later the sirens started blaring."

They were lucky to be alive. Was everybody alive? she wondered, but didn't ask. The answer to that would have to come at another time from another source.

Abby pulled the shirt away. The injury to Reed's perfect back seemed like a personal affront. He could be dead. If whatever hit him had been larger, moving faster... "I'm going to feel around here a bit, but go on."

"How bad is it?"

"I'll let you know soon. The X-rays will tell us more." But after checking the wound,

Abby was fairly certain Reed was going to be fine after a few stitches.

"Anyway. Angus wasn't hurt until he jumped down from the truck and then it was pretty clear he did something to his foot or ankle. I don't think the baby was seriously injured. She was on her mother's lap. The first firemen there convinced Fred to leave because they didn't want him to have a heart attack while they were dealing with the fire. I don't know who else was hurt."

"So you sent Kyle off and stayed."

"I was helping, like everybody else. It was an amazing thing."

"Amazing?"

"Where I come from, most people relegate themselves to gawking. We use our mobile phones to make a call and consider our duty done. The people here ran from their homes and businesses toward the fire."

"They would."

"The chief put most of them to work guarding the perimeter well away from the building, but they were there with buckets of water, shovels and wet towels, anything they thought would keep the fire spreading to the trees."

"They were protecting the town and the

forest. It's just how the people here are."
Abby was never more proud of the residents
of St. Adelbert than she was now, listening to Reed's awestruck story. "They might
gossip and squabble, but they love being a
community."

The tech opened the curtain and pushed in
the portable X-ray machine ahead of him.

Abby put a hand on Reed's shoulder. "I'm
going to put a temporary bandage on for the
X rays." She applied the bandage and hurried
out of the treatment room.

She took a couple big breaths to bring her
emotions under control. Another minute or
two and she thought her heart might actually
break apart. Reed acted like one of the people
of St. Adelbert, not an outsider.

And yet, as it was, his life wasn't here in
this town.

She refused the tears that wanted to form
in her eyes.

"Abby?"

She turned to see Dr. DeVane watching
her.

ALONE IN THE ROOM AFTER the X-rays were
complete, Reed had the time to wonder what

the hell he had been doing. He wasn't kidding about what he would have done if he had been in Chicago.

After the debris had finished falling he'd helped drag, push and carry until everyone was away from the burning building. Cora and Ethel appeared as if out of nowhere and he sent Kyle with them, though the boy wanted to stay with Angus. The obvious thing for Reed to do then was to help the undermanned firefighters until their backup arrived. Second man on the hose took mostly muscle, and in a gym, even a city guy could get that. He didn't have to do it long because the rest of the volunteer firefighters raced in from all directions.

He didn't feel like a hero. He felt like one of the town. He couldn't say he had ever thought about feeling that way about any group of people before.

Or any woman.

No one he'd dated, courted, or seen for any length of time had made him feel as accepted as Abby Fairbanks had. She hadn't hurled herself at whatever image she had conjured of him or tried to make him think he was the only man in the world for her. She had been real.

He remembered the softness of her lips, the firmness of her body. She wasn't afraid to have a little muscle on her either. She looked good in jeans, and he imagined she'd look equally good in a fancy dress, but he doubted the opportunity would come up in St. Adelbert.

"Hi. How are you doing?"

Abby stood in front of him. Seeing her there was like seeing her for the first time. If she lived in Chicago, she would be the kind of woman he thought he could grow to love.

No, he loved her now, his heart told him.

The thought stopped him from speaking and he stared mutely at her.

"Reed, are you okay?"

"I'm fine. I guess lying here with nothing to do leads to deep thoughts."

"Be careful not to hurt yourself." She grinned at him.

"Funny," he said as he felt her grin down into his belly. Abby Fairbanks made him happy.

Dangerous territory. It'd do him in if he ever hurt Abby again.

"Dr. DeVane is putting a cast on someone."

"Angus?"

"Yes, but I can't tell you that." As soon as she finished taking his blood pressure and pulse again, the curtain was pulled back by a tall, and Reed had to grudgingly admit, good-looking man.

"Hello, Mr. Maxwell. I'm Dr. Daley. I'll be reading your X-rays." He then stepped over to look at Reed's wound. "Nurse Fairbanks was just telling me about your exploits."

"I'm sure Nurse Fairbanks exaggerated. Everyone else did."

The doctor gave Abby a long, steady look and she grinned at the man. Reed wondered if that meant anything and wondered if that was a buzz of jealousy he felt in response. That man would be a good catch for Abby. Heck, she'd hardly miss him when he was gone.

"The X-rays are good news."

Reed was disappointed to see the man was better looking when he smiled.

What the hell did he care about the man's smile? "How soon can I get out of here?"

Daley turned to Abby. "How soon, Abby?"

"I'll have him ready for stitches in ten minutes. If everything stays quiet out there."

Daley turned back to Reed. "Soon enough?" Then without waiting for an answer, he nodded to Abby. "I'll be back in ten minutes." And he left.

A FEW HOURS LATER, ABBY picked up debris in the last dirty treatment room. Once the doctor had confirmed Reed's injury was superficial, Abby let herself relax a bit.

Reed had refused pain medication but accepted a ride home from one of the EMTs whose job was finished for the day as long as things remained calm in St. Adelbert.

By eleven-thirty, everyone had been assessed, treated, most had been sent home. They had been lucky. Only the two heating and air-conditioning workers were sent to Kalispell to be hospitalized, and probably just overnight.

It wasn't until the quiet aftermath that Abby realized she hadn't even had a flash of panic. It was gone. Maybe the rest of Denver would fade like that.

Twenty minutes later, Abby stepped into her own kitchen. As soon as she did, she spied a piece of paper on the table. A note. Her mother had taken Kyle home with her.

Abby felt lonely in her own home. She wanted to rush over to her mother's to reassure herself Kyle was all right, but they would be asleep. Instead she flicked on her computer. There was nothing from Lena and the virtual silence took a chunk out of her peace of mind.

Happy thoughts. Think happy thoughts. That's what she told Kyle when he needed to learn how to give himself a boost.

Sleep was out. Going to talk to Reed about Kyle was out. He would be tired after the ordeal and most likely asleep. Tomorrow would be soon enough. Besides, what was she going to say to him now? He was a town hero. Kyle couldn't have a better role model than a man like Reed Maxwell.

The night got a little darker and she got a little lonelier.

She shook her head and pushed up from her chair. There must be some wash to be done. Sure enough, piled on the laundry room floor were Kyle's dirty clothes. She smiled. Apparently, "Gramma" didn't do laundry, either. She put dirty, grass-stained clothing into the washer, almost giddy that there was no blood on them or the smell of smoke.

Light tapping on the back door told her she was not alone in the world. She dried her hands and went to the door.

Through the curtain she could see Reed standing on her back porch. The sight of him upright and smiling had her heart doing unreasonable things, unreasonable especially since the man should be in bed resting.

She pulled open the door.

His hair was messy sexy and his feet were bare. He wore one of Jesse's T-shirts with a rude saying, and she had to admit the rude words had probably never before been so well displayed. He looked like the grown-up version of the boy in the picture, adorable and strong and all man, and she just wanted to grab him and make him...

"Hi," she forced herself to say calmly as she stepped back so he could enter. "How are you feeling?"

He stepped inside and closed the door. He stood looking at her, saying nothing.

The nurse in her, not so long ago set aside for the day, sprang back to life. "Reed, are you okay?"

"I don't think so." His low husky voice said things to Abby the woman, not the nurse.

Before she could reply or ask him what he meant, he lowered his mouth to hers and drew her body against his.

She pushed away. "Reed, what are you doing?"

"Kissing you?"

"You're injured."

"It's a ding on my back."

"It's a bit more than a ding."

"Not to me it isn't." He pulled her against him again and the warmth of his kiss filled her with need. The need to be desirable, the need to feel pleasure, the pleasure a woman and a man could make together. She opened her mouth and let his insistent tongue inside to taste and tease hers.

This time when she pushed away, it was to suggest they not stand in the middle of the kitchen and make out.

"Where should we make out?" Reed demanded with a smirk.

"Somewhere where my neighbors can't see us through the window."

"Maybe they already know your mother bought condoms for us."

"But they don't have to know when we use them."

"Are we going to use them?"

"I hope so."

"Are you sure?"

"Come, I'll show you." She crooked a finger at him.

CHAPTER THIRTEEN

ABBY PLACED REED'S ARM around her, pretending he needed support, and placed his other hand on her hip. As they moved down the hallway toward the stairs, his hand began to rove and caress. The trepidation she had felt under the meteors should still be there, she knew it should, but she couldn't find it anywhere. The fear that he was Kyle's conniving uncle should be there, but it wasn't.

All she could feel was the excitement of being with him.

At the foot of the stairs, he stopped and dipped his head for a lingering kiss that had her breathless. When she wanted more of him, she put her hand under his shirt and reveled in the firm planes of his pecs and the silkiness of his chest hair.

The next she knew, Abby was plastered against the wall, pinned to it in a most delightful manner by Reed's body.

She broke her mouth away from his. "Are you sure you're all right for this?"

"Do I seem all right?"

"You smell like smoke."

"Not me, just my pants. I'm going to see if I can get that nice landlady to do laundry for me like she did for my brother."

"I think she can do that, but that doesn't really answer my question. Are you all right?"

"And I ask again, do I seem all right?"

"You—"

He pressed harder until she could feel the full swell of his erection.

"Um—yes," she said, then grasped his roving hand and started up the stairs. A few steps up Reed stopped.

She turned to see why.

With him a step below, they were nose to nose and he had a serious look on his face. "So what was that between you and that doctor?"

"Which one?"

"Doctor tall and dark."

She laughed. "Dr. Daley. Ah, nothing."

"It seemed like something."

"Okay. So it was. Are you jealous?"

"Should I be?"

"Oh, let's see. He is awfully handsome, smart, rich."

"Just like me."

"Ooh, you're full of yourself, aren't you?" She ran a fingertip along his jaw then around the neckline of his rude shirt. "Well, he lives here in St. Adelbert."

"I guess there is that."

"There's something else."

"There's more?"

"He's married to Dr. DeVane and she's about to have his baby, and they are in the midstages of a tragic and beautiful happily-ever-after love story."

"Do you believe in that?"

"Happily ever after? I think so. I'm just not too sure everyone gets to have it, though." She nudged his nose with hers. "So were you jealous?"

"I might have been."

"What else was between us was—"

"Ah-ha." He nudged back. "I knew there was more."

"Ah-ha yourself. What else was between us was I told him you'd act like one of us, and give him an 'aw shucks' when he talked about you helping people and fighting fires, and he's—well, he's also from Chicago and he said no way." She stepped down until they were both jammed on the same step and pressed tightly against each other. "Anything else?"

"Now that you asked. The undertaker."

She laughed at this. "He and I are through."

Reed drew his eyebrows together.

"He and I know why we were there. We were an excuse to get Kenny and Delanna together. That's all."

"Is there a man in the valley you haven't seen?"

"Hey, I'm their nurse."

He laughed this time. "I asked for that."

"You did. Now is that settled?"

"Yes, but now I have something else that needs to be settled."

She pressed against him creating an unmistakable proposal. "The condoms are upstairs."

"Not all of them." He reached into his pants pocket and pulled out a small packet.

"You came over here with intent." She jammed a fist on her hip in unconvincing outrage.

"And your point is?" He kissed her again, his lips moving, searching, claiming, his hand roving again, caressing her.

"Let's go. Now!" She broke away and ran up the rest of the stairs.

He followed her unhurriedly, his long lean legs flexing, his hand reaching toward her, beckoning. She shook her head slowly from side to side. He grinned at her with a luscious look of anticipation. His hair was getting less and less neat, the front lopped to one side in a casual style, more like the wild Montana mountain man he could be.

He reached for her and she took a quick step back.

"Wait there," she told him and started a slow deliberate strut away from him.

"Are you trying to make me crazy?"

"Ooh, the corporate mogul being forced to cool his—um—jets. Maybe this will help?" She reached for the tail of her shirt, stripped it deliberately over her head, and dropped it on the floor behind her as she continued in a slow strut down the hallway toward her bedroom. A few more steps and she stopped. Her jeans she shimmied down and left on the floor where they had dropped and then she resumed her saunter. Without turning, she reached behind her and unhooked her bra. That she dangled from her fingertips and let drag on the wooden floor of the hallway as she walked toward her room. In the doorway she let it go.

"You're killing me here." His voice was low and dangerous with an underlying growl.

"I just want to make sure you can find your way to me," she said as she disappeared inside. "Wouldn't want the big-city guy to get lost in the Wild West."

His chuckle was a delectable threat.

"You can come now." She waved her panties out the door. "This way."

She had no idea he was so close until he snatched the panties off her fingertip, and reached in to grab her wrist. He held her naked body against him with one hand while he shed his clothing with the other. He moved faster than she ever imagined a one-armed man with a naked woman pressed against him could.

"There are some things that are very similar in the big city and in the Wild West." He dipped his head, she thought he was going to kiss her lips but he reached lower and caught her nipple in his mouth taking a deep drag. She dug her fingers into his dark hair and rode the sensations while he moved to her other breast and then down her belly.

Nothing was more right than this.

"The bed, Reed." Her voice came out in a whispered pant. "I want you…to take me to…bed not…in the doorway."

"Too big city for you?"

"Too confined."

"I like the Wild West more and more all the time."

"You're sure?"

He took half a step back and she was rewarded with the sight of everything she imagined he might be and more. If he had glistened with oil or been deeply tanned, he could not have looked better, and she had absolutely no doubt he could satisfy her every need.

"I can take you in the bed, but not to the bed. The doctor told me not to lift anything heavy for a few days," he said, interrupting her ogle.

"I guess I can't take offense at that." She circled the tip of his eager penis with her finger. "Under the circumstances."

He grabbed her hand and lifted her fingers to his lips. "None intended."

She turned her palm to his and led him to the bed. "I don't want to be the reason you have to see the doctor tomorrow."

She flicked on the bedside lamp, tossed two of her extra pillows lengthwise down the far side of her double bed, and motioned for him to lie down. He lay on his side and grinned up at her as she slid in beside him.

Propped up on one elbow, he began exploring her body with his other hand.

"You're beautiful," he said and then pressed his lips to hers.

Abby used her tongue lovingly to stroke his. She reveled in the feeling of doing something for herself, totally for herself, not worrying about the world.

She slid her hand on Reed's hip and down the sleek muscles of his thigh, then up to the swell of his butt. She caressed everything she could reach that didn't involve a bandage.

When he dipped in with his fingers, she gasped at the exquisite feeling and then leaned over and grabbed a condom, any condom, from her bedside table, ripped the package open and slid the condom in place.

He leaned in and kissed her, but when he started to move over her, she stopped him and pushed him onto his side. "I'm afraid you might hurt something. I've got a better idea."

She faced him and stretched out to fit against the length of his body. Lifting her top leg over his she shifted until he was poised to enter her. She stared into his eyes as she tucked her body against him, taking all of him inside her.

He filled her. She could never want more than him.

"How's that?" The strained words squeaked out of her throat.

He didn't answer, but rocked back and then forward, staring at her until she smiled. With his free hand, he teased her breasts and nipples with his fingers.

He smiled and then kissed her lips and then her nape and murmured something unintelligible at the dip at the base of her neck.

She dropped her head back and sighed. "Yeah, me, too."

Satisfied she wouldn't accidentally hurt him, Abby added her own rhythm. The combination quickly absorbed her.

She let the feelings of pure desire, pure pleasure capture her. She tingled body and soul for this man. She wanted what he would give her, and she trusted him to give her everything she needed.

He moved inside her and she rode the thrill to the brink and then forced herself back. Reed seemed to be with her every step of the way, and when she leaned away to look into his face, he gave her a smoky smile.

Reed Maxwell could take care of himself in bed. Liberation.

It had been so long— No, it had been never. She had never felt so free to feel her own pleasure. She reached around and pressed him farther inside her and he sucked in a quick breath at the added sensation.

She grinned and he thrust deeper.

A sudden demanding, entirely pleasing kind of discontent seized Abby and she moved faster.

"Reed?"

"Go ahead, Abby. Go ahead."

She let the explosion take her. Rushes, exquisite pulsations rocked her and Reed obliged her until he bucked against her one final time.

Then they clung to each other breathing hard, neither wanting to relinquish the moment.

"Mmm," she said after a while as she nuzzled the fine hair of his chest.

"Mmm yourself."

She reached up and flicked off the lamp.

In the blink of darkness that followed it was as if she had, by some mysterious force, flipped another kind of switch. This time when they made love, their desperate need surprised her, but took her even higher than their initial coupling.

Abby wondered how often they could do this in one night and silently hoped they weren't finished yet.

After a while, Reed went to the bathroom and when he returned, they lay side by side, facing each other.

He groaned in the darkness.

"Reed?"

In answer, he groaned again.

"What's the matter?"

"I think I'm going to faint."

She scrambled to her knees, and flicked on the bedside lamp. "Tell me." She started feeling the area around the wound.

"Abby."

"How bad do you feel? Is it the pain?"

"It's the hunger."

She stopped her probing and sat back. "After what we just did? Twice?"

"After, I didn't eat since an early lunch and I don't have any food in the apartment."

She scowled at him. "That was pretty lame, bucko."

"You can make me better by letting me have some of your food."

"I probably should just skin ya and pin yer hide to the barn door fer scarin' me like that."

"You Western folk are pretty harsh." He ran a finger over her lips and she leaned forward and gave him a lingering kiss on the mouth.

"Maybe I'll make us both some food. I've got some bread and cheese and some nice fresh tomatoes. Grilled cheese?"

"Soon?"

She smiled.

"Soon as I find something to put on." She pointed a finger at him. "And, yes, I am going to put clothes on."

"That's no fun."

She slid on her robe. "You can wait here or come down and help. You are the injured hero after all."

He climbed off the bed and crossed the room to where she stood. "I'm conflicted."

"About what?"

"Now I'm hungry in more ways than one."

"Hmm. I'm a trauma nurse. We adapt quickly to changing situations."

He slid his hands inside her robe and pulled her to him. She pressed against him and when he entered her where she stood, she put one leg around his buttocks and pressed him closer, taking as much of him inside as she could get, feeling the pressure of him filling her, stirring her quickly to arousal again.

"Can we try the green fluorescent one this time?" she whispered in his ear and then took a nibble of the lobe.

"I think the green one might be better with a black light."

"It won't see much light, will it?"

"Harsh and demanding," he said as he moved inside her. "And we better get that green one, or any of them, I don't care as long as it's soon."

REED LET THE DROWSINESS flow through him. Beside him Abby breathed softly. She had satisfied his appetite in more ways than one, many times, and he couldn't help wanting her again, forever.

Could he and Abby have a forever? When he tried to picture her in his world, he saw an exquisite flower withering on the stem because it had been cut away from the roots that fed it. He didn't doubt she could hold her own among the people of his world, but he couldn't figure out why she would want to do so.

The mountains and the wide openness of this countryside fed her soul. She had said that that day they had hiked to the waterfall. He had felt the privilege of being allowed a glimpse of how beautiful she was on the inside. He wasn't sure the controlled temperatures and atmosphere of his world could feed her soul in the same way.

He propped himself up on his elbow. Right now, he had her in her world. He touched her breast, pressed his palm against her nipple, and when the bud tightened, she moaned softly.

"I love you, Abby Fairbanks," he whispered

even though he knew he didn't have the right, but he knew there had never been anyone like Abby in his life, never would be.

Would he have to harm Nurse Fairbanks? He had to leave and if Kyle was Jesse's son—he had to bring the boy back to Chicago to his other grandmother. He would have to rip apart one woman's existence to mend another's.

The DNA sample from Kyle was stashed in the pocket of his pants, which were lying on the floor, and seemed to be calling out to him.

Traitor.

To whom?

To his brother, his mother, Kyle?

Abby?

A NEW MORNING. ABBY PACED her kitchen while Reed slept upstairs in her bed. She hoped she hadn't broken her own heart to have sex, glorious sex, better than she had ever had in her life sex, I'm going to want it every day for the rest of my life sex with Reed Maxwell.

Reed Maxwell might not be the enemy, but he could actually take Kyle away. His was a world totally different than what Kyle was used to. She got a stark image of Kyle looking around at everything new again and completely unknown. Kyle wouldn't remember the move from Denver.

She did. She remembered the final act that had sent her fleeing with her family. At the trial, the resident doctor who had administered the incorrect dose of medication to the woman had turned and pointed at her as the wrongdoer. The hospital, because it had deep pockets, had taken the financial hit and to mollify the family had fired her.

All during the trial reporters had hounded her until Kyle cried in her arms. After the verdict that said she was guilty of the mistake—that's what they called it, a tragic mistake—she ran for the last time, home, when she packed up her family and left the city.

Reed wasn't the enemy. Her wounded psyche was. She had trapped herself in this tiny part of the universe. Maybe she could leave? Maybe she could move to Chicago? He hadn't asked but she was sure he would. He had whispered he *loved* her when he thought she was asleep.

She shivered as she paced through to the

living room and back to the kitchen. She had checked on word from or about Lena, but there was still nothing.

Wednesday, 6:00 a.m. the clock on her stove said. Two more days to work this week and she had to be at the clinic in two hours. She had showered and pulled her damp hair into a limp ponytail. Time for coffee. While the pot brewed she paced some more. Then she remembered Reed saying that maybe his "nice landlady" would wash his pants. She knew he wouldn't even blink if she said no and maybe that's why she wanted to wash his clothes for him.

Quietly she nabbed the rude shirt and pants from the floor of her room. When she pressed her nose into the shirt, all she smelled was him, no smoke. She sniffed again. The two of them had been so delightfully wanton. She hadn't ever been wanton before. Wanted to be again soon.

In the laundry room she started the machine filling and added the detergent. Automatically she checked the pockets of his pants. Good thing, too. She found the key to his rental car, some change, a small plastic bag and a vinyl glove. She put the small handful of things on the counter beside the washing machine and put the clothing in the washer.

It wasn't until she closed the lid that she picked up the glove that had partially obscured the contents of the plastic bag. Sealed inside the bag was a pair of cotton-tipped swabs.

It was an odd thing for Reed to have.

It looked like a throat culture or a—DNA sample.

Her sun crashed into her earth.

CHAPTER FOURTEEN

WITHOUT EVEN ASKING, Reed planned to check Kyle's paternity.

When he had the proof, real proof, not just an anecdotal picture, he could use his money and influence to take Kyle away any time it pleased him.

She wiped at the tears and sat down at the kitchen table. She had to think of Kyle. He loved Reed. If she fought for custody, it would only break Kyle's heart. If couched in the right way, maybe she could get Kyle to want to go to Chicago. She could even go with him, if it came to keeping peace and tranquillity in the boy's world.

Lena would be destroyed.

Abby's mind whirled and grasped for solutions. Maybe if she relented, Reed's family would only seek temporary custody until Lena got out of the army.

Whatever was going to happen to Kyle, it

was best if she had a hand in administering it. She would see that the boy was protected from any sudden frightening changes and allowed to have as much power and input as possible.

She slipped on her work clothes from the laundry room, grabbed her purse and let herself inside the garage. Once she was in her SUV, she called her mother.

"What the hell, Abby. It's early." Her mother's voice croaked over the phone.

"Mom." She had to swallow to loosen the tightness.

"Abby, what's wrong?"

"I need a favor."

"What's the favor?" her mother asked cautiously.

"I need you, Mom. I need you to keep Kyle close today. I need you to keep him away from—" she drew in a breath for the courage she was going to need "—away from Reed."

"What's going on?"

"Mom, I failed Lena."

"Now what are you talking about, honey? Wait. Wait. Wait, Abby. I hear a great big again in your voice, and I just want to get something perfectly clear. You have *never* failed Lena. You have never been responsible for Lena. Lena is. She is responsible for getting pregnant, for the drugs, for whatever and everything she's done."

"It's just that—"

"It's just that you can't let go. And speaking of feeling responsible, since you got me up before hell thawed, you're going to listen to me, so hear me this time. You did not make your father leave."

Abby inhaled sharply. "What makes you think I—"

"You don't think asking a million times after your father left how you could get him to come back wasn't a clue? You still think it's your fault, don't you?"

Abby had thought she had made her father leave, but that was in the past, wasn't it? She remembered his face as he glared at her and then turned and walked out the door as if it had all happened in just that moment. The pain was real and still strong enough to make her heart ache and her six-year-old hands tremble.

"You're right, Mother." But she wasn't six anymore and she wasn't responsible for the actions of any adult, her father, Lena, Jesse, Reed, her mother, no adult except herself. But she had to learn to let go like her mother said.

"Damn straight I'm right. Now, just lighten up and live your life the best that you can. That's all any of us can do."

Now her mother was reading her mind. "Mom, I just need you to keep a close eye on Kyle today."

"This has something to do with Jesse being Kyle's father, doesn't it?"

"It does."

"Well, Lena sure as hell is responsible for not telling Jesse he was Kyle's father, if that's the case, but I'm not sure it makes a difference who his father is, in the long run, since Jesse has never cared one way or the other."

"It might, Mom. Lena's unit is way overdue and Jesse has been declared missing in Utah."

"Why do you do that, Abby? Why?" Her mother sounded more exasperated than angry.

"Keep stuff from you?"

Her mother scoffed. "My God, honey. Why do you keep stuff all to yourself? Why do you think you've got to take the troubles of the world on, by yourself, and not share the load?"

"I thought you liked that about me."

"I understand that's what you do, but I'm not sure I ever liked it. Now tell me about Lena and Jesse."

Abby explained about Lena's squad not having checked in and Jesse being officially declared missing by the state of Utah, and finding the DNA swab.

"They wouldn't take Kyle to Chicago, would they? He's so settled here." Her mother spoke with fear in her tone. "They wouldn't take a little boy away from his family."

"They might be his family, too."

"Kenny wanted to take me boating on the reservoir today, and he invited Kyle to go with us. I wasn't sure it was a good idea, so I said maybe another time, but…"

"Kenny wanted to take you out? Way to go, Mom."

"He's so nice and so sexy, Abby. I hated turning him down."

"Well, call him and tell him you changed your mind and that Kyle will love it." And the reservoir was far enough away from St.

Adelbert that Reed would not find them on his own.

"I'll keep Kyle safe, Abby. You can depend on me."

The sincerity in her mother's tone made another teardrop fall down onto Abby's cheek. Her mother was a changed woman. She would not let Kyle down, and Kenny Fuller was a fool if he didn't fall head over heels in love with Delanna Fairbanks.

Abby closed the call and started her car. She'd go visit the mountains before work. She might have to leave them soon.

REED STOOD IN THE DOORWAY of Abby's kitchen dressed in a towel. His clothes had been missing when he got up and his worst fear was realized when he heard the washing machine running. He couldn't care less that Abby might have washed the sample. Barely a thing would have been lost if she had. Collecting it had been cheap and easy and in retrospect, stupid.

But she had found it. Abby must feel as if someone had stabbed her in the back. Just like he felt. The big difference was, all he needed to recover was time and a little prudent care.

The kind of wound he had inflicted on her might never fully heal.

The sight of the empty spot in the garage where her car had been caused an equally empty spot in his chest. He never meant to hurt people. He was much better with hard data. Data was cold and without feeling and he wondered if he had become like that. He turned away from the doorway to go check the progress of his laundry.

After he tossed the clothes into the dryer, he paced the house for a while, stopping from time to time to very gently stretch the injured muscles of his back. He wished he had his laptop. He didn't want to boot Abby's computer and invade her private space any more than he already had.

When seven-thirty finally rolled around, he sat down on the couch and called Denny at the office.

Reed was relieved and oddly pleased. The issue with the client had been ironed out. The land had been purchased at a fairly reasonable price, and it looked like smooth sailing from now on and the biggest deal they had ever brokered.

"And we're getting along quite nicely

without you. Take all the time you need," Denny told him.

All the time you need. Forever had a nice feel to it. Maybe letting Denny have more control would help him in a lot of ways.

"I have some more information for you."

"What do you have?"

"I sent our P.I. to Denver—"

"You sent our P.I. to Denver?" Reed sat up straight on the couch, ignoring the stab of pain in his back. He pinched the bridge of his nose.

"Yeah, he said—"

"Denny, stop." That was what Abby had meant the other day by the river. He didn't know if he wanted to find out anything about Abby's past. She must already feel he'd betrayed her trust, but the boy's welfare might be at stake and he'd listen. If someone had been interested in the welfare of two poor little rich boys, Jesse might not be lost and maybe dead right now. "Go on. What did he find out?"

"Well, I'll apologize in advance for this. What I have isn't going to make your life any easier."

Reed slumped shoulders he didn't even

realize he had been tensing. "What do you have?"

"I think you should read the report. There's a lot here and you'll have to make up your own mind about what it means."

He trusted Denny's instincts. "You sent it?"

"It should be in your in-box."

The next couple minutes was spent talking about Reed's mother and about how Denny was working around Reed's absence quite well. Then Reed disconnected the call.

When he slipped on the pants and shirt from the drier, they were warm but still damp, good enough to get him to the apartment without giving the neighbors a view of the city guy in a towel.

Once in the apartment, he changed into dry clothes and hung the damp ones on the back of the kitchen chairs in the sunshine. Then he downloaded the information Denny had sent. The sections on court records got Reed's attention first. He leaned toward the computer's screen as if it would help him understand words that didn't seem to fit with the Abby Fairbanks he knew so well.

No wonder she had fled the city. If she

thought he planned to take Kyle to Chicago, it must have her frightened out of her mind.

He wanted to hold her in his arms again, but that couldn't lead to anything except more heartache for all of them.

He had been reading and digesting the information from Denny for a couple of hours when his phone rang.

"Good morning, Mother."

The conversation went as most of his conversations with his mother went.

It wasn't until he hung up that he realized he should try to see the human side of her. She was self-centered and totally dependent on the people around her. Until she sobered up, she had never put any time or effort into being a parent. If there was a mother who deserved to have her children turn their backs on her, it was Frieda Hale Maxwell. Now that she was sober, she wished she had a family and seemed to think wishing should make it so.

He couldn't help think of another woman who wasn't a mother, but should be. Abby. She had every reason to reject the world, to be withdrawn and bitter, to turn inward and think only of herself. She had more reasons than most to complain about how unfair life was, but she didn't.

Maybe his mother, who had no reason to be selfish and demanding could be more like Abby—if someone gave her the chance. Maybe there was more humanity in his mother than the people around her gave her credit for. He vowed to try to find it when he got home.

And it was time to go home, to get out of town before he caused any more pain to any more people. He wasn't a complete heel, though. He'd wait for Abby to come home from work and he'd wish her well. She deserved it. She deserved every good thing that came into her life.

CHAPTER FIFTEEN

FOR ABBY, THE DAY HAD been long and yet not long enough to find any real answers. She got out of her car and slowly climbed the stairs to the apartment she had rented to brothers who seemed to separately conspire to break her heart. One because he was so irresponsible and one because he was the opposite.

When she got to the landing, she turned and sat down. She couldn't bring herself to knock. She had hoped she could figure out what she was going to say, hoped making herself climb the stairs would somehow force her to find the words, the right questions. Her mother and Kyle were still not home and now would be the best time to put all the cards on the table.

Having Reed say out loud what he had planned would be so final, and now that she was there, she wasn't sure she wanted to hear it.

She put her elbows on her knees and chin her in her hands. She might not be a mother, but she'd be the best damned aunt in the world.

Now she was afraid an aunt just wasn't enough.

I'm sorry, Kyle, she thought. *I'm so sorry.*

Lena—she pictured her sister in her camouflage ACU's, Army Combat Uniform, grinning the day she graduated from boot camp, and Abby prayed she'd see that grin again—*if you're safe, I'm going to kick your butt all around the town when I see you.*

Through the interminably long workday she was at least able to convince herself Reed Maxwell still had no evil intent. This time, like it or not, she had been able to see all sides.

She had spent the day burying herself in patient care and paperwork. When either of those flagged, she'd started calling patients who had been seen the previous week and who might benefit from or just like a follow-up call.

Now she had to confront the man who could trash her world.

Well, enough of this.

She stood, hoping for boldness she didn't feel, and immediately saw Reed in the doorway. Funny, he didn't look any different than he had yesterday morning. He didn't look any more devious, any more sexy, any more of anything, except maybe he looked a little sad, tired, with a day and a half's growth of beard.

He hadn't slept any more than she had last night.

"Hello, Abby. Would you like to come in?"

She tried to read any message in his words, but the invitation was polite, nothing more. Maybe that was the message. Civility could reign between them. All they had to do was keep any feelings out of their predicament.

"I came to invite you to come over for a cup of tea," she said, trying to sound calm, though her heart was breaking.

Reed nodded and he followed her down the steps.

They sat at her kitchen table in the light of the late-afternoon sun talking of things that meant little as if by a silent agreement they had decided to wait for the tea to be ready before they said what they had to say.

When the water was hot, and the tea steeping in mugs, Abby folded her hands on the tabletop and studied his face for any sign of emotion. There was only the steady look of interest. Maybe the kind a cobra gives its prey. Well, during the day she'd built up her resistance to anything he would hand out.

She loved him, or she loved the man she wanted in her life, the man who cared about the people around him enough to fight a fire for them. The man who laughed at the same things she laughed at, who appreciated the bounty Montana's nature had to offer. The man who instinctively knew her well enough to give her the gift of a meteor shower.

"What if Kyle is Jesse's son?" Abby didn't realize she was going to blurt that out, but she knew it was best gotten out on the table, so to speak.

Reed's steady gaze flickered a little and he took a sip of what had to be weak tea from his cup. "But we don't know that for sure."

He was playing with her, testing. "Well, there's the picture you have."

He continued to gaze steadily. Eventually the corners of Reed's mouth turned up and Abby wondered what that meant. She didn't dare let herself hope.

"There are things about Kyle that reminded me of Jesse when Jesse was a kid. The blond curls, the way he runs, and Jesse had a dimple when he was a kid, like Kyle does now. So I had a picture of Jesse sent to me."

Somehow the information lightened her heart. "You didn't already know when you got here. You didn't bring the picture with you."

"I didn't know and not say anything?" He challenged her with his eyes. "Did you?"

She expelled a breath of relief and shook her head. "Lena would never tell me who Kyle's father was. It wasn't until I saw the picture that I had any real proof."

He nodded.

"Did you have a private investigator asking questions about me in Denver?" she asked without letting her gaze waver.

He frowned, but didn't answer.

"You have to think about it?"

"Yes, in a way."

"I thought that was a yes or no question."

She pulled the tea bag out of her cup and squeezed it against her spoon.

"My business partner, Denny, is helping me search for Jesse. He sent the investigator we use to find out about prospective customers and the veracity of their assets."

He didn't know about Kyle before he got here. He wasn't snooping into her past, not really. Suddenly the last vestiges of her anger at herself, at him, at everyone fled. She wanted to leap out of her chair and throw her arms around his neck, but there seemed to be more he was not yet telling her. She stayed sitting tight in her chair.

"You were right," she said as she took a sip of tea.

"About what?"

"We are alike in some ways. In the way our siblings seem to make their problems ours."

He nodded. "Jesse must know. How could he live so close to his own son and not know."

"Maybe he's no better at figuring out such things than you are, than I am."

"Maybe." He gave her a faint smile. "It might be too late for this."

"Jesse's not dead. I won't believe anything except that he's alive and coming back."

"I didn't mean that." He reached into his pocket. When he brought his hand back out and put it on the tabletop, he was holding the plastic bag with the samples in it.

"You're giving this to me now? Why?"

He reached for her hand.

"I did not come here to destroy a family." He looked into her eyes and she knew his words came from his heart. "I came to try to mend one. I spoke with my mother this afternoon, and to be perfectly honest, if it was up to me whether Kyle stayed here with you, happily oblivious to the fact that he had another family, or came back to Chicago to meet my family, I'd choose that he stay here for a long time."

Abby could barely breathe. "Who is it up to?"

"Jesse, if he comes back, or Lena, if she comes back. If they don't come back, then it's up to you and someday, up to Kyle."

Kyle could stay here. Tears pressed at the back of her eyes and an aching lump filled her throat.

"I have to go. I waited until you got home

to speak with you. Thank you for all you've done. Thank you for being the great person you are, the good aunt."

He got up from the table, releasing her hand to come around and kiss her on the right cheek. He walked out the door.

Abby sat in the middle of her kitchen dumbfounded.

Through the window, she watched Reed go up to the apartment. He went inside and a moment later, he appeared on the landing with his jacket and his laptop in his hand.

He was leaving? He was just leaving?

She heard his car back out and pull away. It was over, all over. Reed was gone forever. Kyle was safe.

All the worrying and now Kyle was safe and Reed was leaving her alone. What she thought she wanted felt deeply hollow, and she knew immediately there was no way she could, in good conscience, keep Kyle away from his other family. She would make sure the acquaintance took place at Kyle's pace, giving him the news slowly, in pieces he could handle. She would do all she had fought against, but slowly.

How she would tell him anything about his parents being missing, she had no idea.

She started to laugh. Her own laughter made her laugh more until she released the cup and put her hands over her face.

Nothing left in her life was funny and all she could do was laugh. She had only an empty ache in her heart and all she could do was laugh, meaninglessly.

Then, when she had laughed all she could laugh, she didn't know what was she supposed to do now, so she put her head down on the table and closed her eyes.

A knock startled her awake. She sat up blinking and then jumped up from the chair.

REED DROVE UP MAIN STREET in the middle of St. Adelbert for the last time. He pulled into the clinic, where Dr. Daley met him at the door. The two men shook hands.

"Thanks for checking my back before I left town and for waiting to see me after the clinic closed."

"How's your back feeling today?"

"Like someone kicked me."

Dr. Daley led Reed inside the clinic and into one of the treatment rooms.

"Slip your shirt off and I'll take a look at it," he said and then washed his hands at the sink across the room and dried them on a clean cloth towel.

Reed took his shirt off and sat on the stool where Dr. Daley had pointed, in the same treatment room where Abby had so meticulously cared for him yesterday—a lifetime ago.

"I'm afraid the tape coming off is going to be the worst. Are you sure you need to leave town tonight? You'd be much better off staying a couple more days or at least finding someone to drive you to the airport in Kalispell."

Before Reed got a chance to answer, Dr. Daley pulled off the dressing.

He took in a sharp breath and then answered. "It's best if I leave sooner than later."

"There are other benefits to staying in town longer, like basking in the praise of these kindly townsfolk." Dr. Daley gently probed the area around the wound. "More than one of them would probably like to thank you for pitching in at the auto shop. I'm going to listen to your lungs now."

"I'm afraid I have already fallen from grace with the townspeople."

Dr. Daley leaned back and looked at him with a knowing smile. "Fast work, city fella. What did you do to Abby?"

Reed snorted softly. "Enough to be lynched, I'm afraid."

Reed felt the telltale cold of a stethoscope as Dr. Daley placed it on his upper back. "Take a deep breath—use your mouth rather than your nose."

He repeated the process until he was satisfied. "Sounds good. Abby tells me you're from Chicago. How did you adapt to living out here?" Reed asked as Daley showed him a percussion hammer and began testing the reflexes on the lower part of his body, presumably to make sure there had been no trauma to the spinal cord that had not shown up yesterday.

"It was more realizing this was the place I needed to be rather than adapting to it."

Reed thought of how the drive through the mountains with Abby had seemed more like coming home than being a tourist on a day trip. "Being here is like nothing I've ever known before," Reed admitted to the doctor.

"Be careful. That's how it starts. Throw in a woman who could tear your heart to shreds, but who chooses instead to love you and you get an offer you can't turn down."

"I don't think I have to worry about the second part. I crossed the line one too many times."

Daley stood thinking, tapping the palm of his own hand with the rubber hammer.

"Did you kiss her to prove she wasn't good enough to date your brother?"

"No." That was an odd question.

"Did you insult and embarrass her on her first day of residency so she almost quit medicine?"

"I did not do that." Reed was starting to see where Daley was pointing the light, but it couldn't matter.

"Well, then. Did you accuse her of helping your niece become a juvenile delinquent?"

"*Her* wouldn't be Dr. DeVane would it?"

Daley grinned. He didn't have to answer.

"She must be a saint."

Daley threw his head back and laughed.

"She is a very forgiving woman. Funny thing is, the only thing I had to do was to believe her when she said none of it mattered because she knew why I had done it."

"How well do you know Abby Fairbanks?"

"She's a very forgiving woman."

It was Reed's turn to laugh, only his was more of derision directed at himself. "I didn't give her the chance. I couldn't believe she wanted one."

"She's too good for you."

Reed snapped his gaze up to see Daley smiling. "That's probably true. She faced a whole boardroom full of administrators and physicians and never backed down when they accused her of nearly killing someone and then she faced a judge and a courtroom full of people who also accused her."

Daley raised his eyebrows.

"No, I don't believe she did it." Reed answered the unspoken question quickly enough to surprise even himself.

Daley nodded. "I'm going to rebandage this and I want you to keep it clean and dry for three days. Then have it checked again.

Take the antibiotics I gave you until they are all gone. And you need to talk to her."

"I need to leave her alone."

"For what it's worth to you, my wife says you're an idiot if you walk away. Take it from another idiot—she might be right." When Reed gave him a questioning look, Daley shrugged and lifted one shoulder. "You'd be surprised how much you've been the topic of conversation in this valley. Stay here and you'll give them something to talk about in the grocery store for a long time."

Take all the time you need, Denny had said and he had thought *forever had a nice feel to it.* He hadn't taken the time to wonder where that came from. Maybe he should.

ABBY SAT AT HER KITCHEN table admiring the large bouquet of flowers in the beautiful old vase. Her mother had given her the vase and it was apparently her grandmother's, the only object Abby had that connected her to her ancestors.

Travis Fuller had stopped in and brought the flowers.

They had made small talk for a few minutes. He told her the explosion had been caused by a propane leak and had nothing to do with Fred. The fire chief's preliminary investigation showed a possible faulty valve.

She told him about the extent of the injuries as a result of the blast. He said he knew, because everywhere he went there was a lot of backslapping and smiles that no one had been seriously hurt. Even the men who had been sent to Kalispell had been discharged.

At first Abby had been afraid she would have to find a way to let Travis down gently. As it turned out, Travis was here to let her down as easily and as politely as he could, with a big beautiful bouquet of flowers.

After they laughed about how their parents had used them and then about how their parents hadn't needed to use them at all because Delanna and Kenny seemed to be made for each other, Travis shook her hand and left.

The flowers were beautiful. They were light and fragrant and gorgeous colors. Maybe she should be feeling sad that Travis didn't want her? He was so obviously a very sensitive man.

She was still admiring her flowers when she heard more footsteps on her back porch.

How she ever thought she'd be lonely in this town, she had no idea. When she opened the door this time, it was to a stranger.

CHAPTER SIXTEEN

THE CLEAN-SHAVEN MAN with short dark hair smiled at her. "I hear you're looking for me."

It took Abby another fast assessment of the man in the belted khaki pants and striped dress shirt before she recognized him. The lower half of his face was lighter than the rest as if he'd recently shaved his beard.

"Oh, my God! Jesse! What happened to you?" She held out her arms and he stepped into them.

"Am I still welcome?"

"Of course you are."

He hugged her hard. "Is my brother still here?"

"You heard about that, too."

"Sheriff Potts called me when the Utah Highway Patrol told him I was in Boulder again."

"Why didn't you call me?"

"Do I ever?"

"No, but you should."

"I will from now on. Promise. Being alone in Escalante helped me get my priorities together and I just wanted to get back here."

"Come in. Come in." She tugged on his hand and pulled him into the kitchen.

"Is Kyle here? I missed him."

"He missed you, too." *He made your brother come down and eat butter eggs with us,* she thought. It was a bad idea and she had loved every minute of it. "He went with my mother, boating on the reservoir with Kenny Fuller. They should be back at her house anytime now."

He rubbed his naked chin. "Kyle boating, your mother and the funeral director, many things have changed. Nice flowers."

"Thanks." She told him about Lena's unknown status, about the explosion at the auto shop. He reacted, concerned and shocked, as she thought he would. She looked for any special reaction regarding Lena, but deep friendly concern was all he offered. She didn't tell him about the DNA sample or the photograph of him and Reed. Later. She finally asked, "What brought you out of the park now?"

"Somebody stole my stuff."

"They didn't steal your stuff. They were collecting clues. They thought you might be, um—"

"Dead. Well, I'm not."

"Clearly."

"Got any food?"

"Always." She hugged him again. "It's so good to see you. Hot dogs with cheese?" She couldn't make grilled cheese, not today. Not after sitting at this table consuming melty grilled cheese sandwiches with Reed.

"Mmm. Sounds good. I'm finished bumming from you, though." He pulled out a roll of cash, put it on the table and pushed it toward her.

"Whoa." She waved the money away. "Thanks, but your brother already paid your rent."

"Did he, now? Where is he, by the way?"

Abby's steps faltered and she dropped the knife she had in her hand.

"I'll drag him out into the backcountry and leave him for the bears. What did my excruciatingly responsible brother do to you?"

"Oh, stop it. He was here on important business."

"Convince me."

"Jesse." She sat down at the table and picked up his hand. "Apparently your mother wants to apologize to you."

He frowned and leaned on his forearms. "I've heard that before."

"This time she's sober. She has been for about a year." She told him about his mother realizing she had neglected her family and about her wanting to make it up to her sons.

"So he wasn't here to drag me back to work for the family business. Huh. There's no Ritz-Carlton here, so where is he staying?"

"He was staying at your place, but he's gone now."

"You didn't tell me what he did to you."

"Nothing, really." Just let her break her heart over him. Nothing, really, except go back to his life after making her believe what a great guy he could be—so much better than anything she had found in the St. Adelbert valley or anywhere else. "And you didn't tell me where you were when you didn't pick up your food that guy left for you."

"A hiker got hurt. He couldn't drive. His

fiancée couldn't drive a stick shift, so I helped get him to their car and drove them home to Salt Lake."

"You left your stuff behind." She knew it sounded like an accusation, but it was just worry and she knew Jesse knew that, too.

"I had a day pack and we were a lot closer to their car than my stuff. I know I should have called, but I planned on being back before the food drop." He held up his thumb. "This is not the most reliable mode of transportation to use to cross Utah, especially since it's illegal there."

Reed could be halfway to Interstate 90 by now, because he wasn't hitchhiking. Too bad he had missed his brother's arrival.

"Abby." Jesse tugged the curly lock at the side of her face. "You keep going out on me. You're thinking about him, aren't you?"

She looked into Reed's brother's eyes. She'd never realized how much they looked alike. It must have been the beard. "I was." She clicked her tongue and gave a wistful sigh.

"Your turn. What did he do?"

"He was an ass who didn't have his head on straight."

They both looked up to see Reed standing in the doorway.

Abby froze like a deer in the headlights. She had never seen anything that looked so good. His face was covered with whiskers, his hair was tousled and his clothes rumpled, and she hardly dared to breathe for fear she'd wake up from the beautiful dream.

Jesse got up and shook his brother's hand and then after a minute's hesitation, the two men hugged.

Reed grimaced when his brother squeezed, but said, "Who are you and what have you done with my scraggly brother?"

"Check this out." Jesse turned to Abby but pointed back at his brother. "I'm the clean-shaven one. I'm not sure that's ever happened in our lives."

"Hasn't happened since he could grow whiskers." Reed spoke and the deep thrum of his voice thrilled through Abby and set her heart trembling.

She smiled but she couldn't find anything to say. She didn't know what having Reed standing in her doorway meant. It could mean he had heard his brother was here. Heck, it could mean he forgot his toothbrush. He wasn't here to whisk Kyle away, of that she was sure.

For a brief moment, she wished he hadn't come back. His being here could mean she got to break her heart even more.

The next second, she was elated to see him one more time.

Jesse glanced at Abby and then at Reed and then cocked his head a little to the side as if making a decision. "I'm tempted to hang around, just to torture the two of you, but there is obviously something unfinished between you. Even I'm bright enough to figure that out. I'm outta here. I'm going to the diner and then to your mom's to wait for Kyle to show up."

Reed and Abby exchanged meaningful looks.

"He knows," Abby said when they were alone.

Reed walked slowly across the kitchen toward her. The closer he got, the harder it was for her to take in a breath. By the time he reached her, she couldn't even feel her lips—until he lowered his to them.

He kissed her softly and then stepped away. "Abby, I am so sorry I left."

"It might have been easier on all of us." She couldn't believe she was saying this. It might make him turn around and walk back out the door. "You know, the clean break thing."

"That's just it. I don't want any kind of break." His expression was almost pleading with her to understand him.

She gave a weak smile that probably conveyed the confused thoughts running rampant inside her head. "I don't want a break, either, but eventually that's what is going to happen. Reed, I don't know that it will be any easier next week or next month."

"That's what I'm trying not very well to say. It only has to be today or next week or next month if you say it does."

He'd put it on her. She took several steps away from him. She had to think more clearly, and she couldn't do that when all she had to do to touch paradise was to reach out her hand. They could stay together if she came to the Midwest with him. She had to be the one to decide.

"Wait." He put up his hand. "Whatever it is you heard me say, that's not what I mean."

He moved toward her and she nearly panicked. "I can't do it, Reed."

"Can't do what?"

"I can't leave. Maybe someday, but I can't leave now. You don't understand. This valley gave me my life back. I left once and now I've made something of myself."

"You were a trauma nurse in Denver, I know," he said quietly.

"And for my hard work, they threw me under a bus, a great big one filled with doctors and board members. That resident nearly killed somebody and then he lied and I got fired and a big blot on my record. When I returned here, Dr. DeVane—" She squeezed the edge of the cold, stainless-steel sink and swallowed to relieve the tightness forming in her throat. "Dr. DeVane and Dr. Daley took me on at the clinic without batting an eye because they believed in me when I—"

"Come here." He reached out and pried her away from the counter and wrapped his arms around her.

She put her cheek on his chest and continued, "When I wasn't sure what to believe anymore. They asked me what the truth was, I told them and they hired me."

They stood in the middle of her kitchen without speaking for a long while. He held her tight against him as she clung to the dreams of what it could be like.

"I don't want to leave, either," he said after a while.

"This place can get to you like that."

"I don't mean, 'I don't want to leave but adios.' I mean I would like you to ask me to stay."

Abby held her breath again. Ask him to stay?

"You're thinking too hard. I'm not sure I like that," he said with his lips in her hair.

"Stay. If all I have to do to get you to stay is to ask you, then please stay."

"Now, was that so hard?"

"Can you possibly mean that?"

"Can you possibly fall in love with me the way I've fallen in love with you?"

"I—um—I already have."

"Then say it. I'll go first. I love you, Abby."

"I love you, Reed. But—"

His lips stopped her from talking. "Just a simple 'I love you' will do, no buts."

"How about a 'so'?"

"That might be all right."

"So, what's this about you wanting to stay in St. Adelbert?"

"No. Wait. You asked me to stay and you are not taking that back." He hugged her tightly.

"I wouldn't dream of taking it back. But what about your business?"

"Egotist that I am, I thought the company wouldn't be able to get along without my being there to push and prod and keep things in order, but Denny is having a great time and he's doing a great job."

"I thought you loved making billion-dollar corporate deals, buying and selling businesses and continents."

"It pays the bills. Maintains the family image. And I do it because someone has to do it."

"Oh, please. I've seen your eyes light up when you talked about putting together big deals."

"That part is fun. Anyway, I do most of the research on the computer. I fly all over the world. The commute to the airport is only a little longer from here than it is from the Loop in Chicago."

"You really mean you want to live here?"

"I told you, you asked and you can't take it back."

"Live here?"

"I love you, Abby."

"Live here and you love me? Am I dreaming?"

"Do you want me to pinch you?"

"Maybe you should kiss me."

And he did, long and soft, and then demanding and then down her neck and onto her shoulder.

She pulled back. "Neighbors."

He laughed. "Maybe they should all get used to this."

Later, by the time the pounding started on Abby's back door, they were out of bed and out of the shower and heading down to find some food.

Abby opened the back door and Kyle, her mother, Jesse and Kenny piled into her kitchen, laughing at something extremely humorous.

Kenny was carrying a big bag and Abby realized good smells were coming from it. Delanna started to bring containers of food out of the bag and Jesse was pulling plates and glasses from the cupboard.

Kyle grabbed a glass from the table. "Can I have pop?"

"Milk." Jesse said before anyone else could.

Abby, Reed and Delanna all looked at each other and laughed. Kyle laughed but he liked to laugh, so just having other people laughing was enough for him to start.

The ringing of the phone interrupted the conversation.

Abby grabbed for the phone, hoping it wasn't another emergency. "Hello."

The person on the other end said something, but Abby couldn't quite hear.

"Who?" Abby waved for everyone to be quiet.

"Your sister, you creep. You don't even recognize my voice."

"Lena." That shut everyone up. "Lena, it's so good to hear the sound of your voice."

"Mommy!"

Kyle grabbed for the phone and Abby willingly gave it to him.

Kyle kept shaking his head and nodding.

Abby smiled at how rapt he was at the sound of his mother's voice. "Talk to her, sweetie. She can't hear you shaking your head."

He kept shaking and nodding, but he added the yeses and noes and a giggle from time to time.

His mother must have told him to pass the phone to someone else, because he shoved it at his grandmother and dived into the chicken and mashed potatoes she had scooped onto a plate for him.

By the time the phone came back to Abby, everyone else, even Reed and Kenny, had said hello.

"Jesse's brother? Way to go, Abbs. And Mom has a guy? Guess I should have gotten out of the way sooner."

Abby stepped into the hallway for privacy.

"Lena, I think Jesse knows."

Lena went silent. Neither sister had to ask or explain.

"But it's okay." Abby hurried to reassure her sister. "He just got back from Utah and the very first person he asked about was Kyle."

Another pause.

"Are you sure he's changed?"

"He even talks different. He sounds more like his brother now. He looks more like his brother now. It's as if he wants to be a part of a family now."

There was another long pause.

"Have him tell Kyle if he wants to." Lena spoke softly and didn't say what they were both thinking. It would be good for Kyle to have one parent around, especially if something happened.

"I'll talk to Jesse, but I'm always here for all of you, sis."

"I know, Abbs. I know. You're the best. Gotta go. This card is about to run dry."

"I love you, sis."

The phone line went dead, but Abby could still feel the connection. Lena was alive.

Jesse was alive. Reed loved her.

"Holy cow."

"Holy cow, what?" her mother asked from behind her.

"I can't believe this day. I can't believe my life, your life." She elbowed her mother and looked at Kenny sitting at her kitchen table with the other guys. They looked as if they gathered like that all the time. Maybe they would. "How's it going with Kenny?"

"Well, let's just say, one of these nights, I am not volunteering to babysit and if there's a hankie tied to the front door handle, don't come a knockin'.

"And you?" Her mother put an arm around Abby's shoulder and squeezed.

"Reed wants to stay. I'm not sure of any of the details, but I love him, Mom, and he loves me. Can you believe it?"

"I can, dear, I can."

Reed got up from the table and came over to where Abby and Delanna were standing. "We're getting kind of lonely over there all by ourselves. We could use the company of some beautiful women."

Delanna preened at his words and sashayed away.

Abby smiled at him and her heart filled with more love than she ever thought a heart could hold and the whole world seemed to glow. She'd finally found a way to see the good in everything.

"Yes."

"Yes, what?" He pushed her curls back from her face.

"You asked me if I believed in happily ever after."

He leaned in and kissed her and when they looked up, everyone cheered.

* * * * *